Franz Grillparzer
THE JEWESS OF TOLEDO

GERMAN CLASSICS

Franz Grillparzer

THE JEWESS
OF TOLEDO

AN HISTORICAL TRAGEDY
IN FIVE ACTS

With an introduction
by
William Guild Howard

MONDIAL

Mondial
New York

Franz Grillparzer:
The Jewess of Toledo

German original title: "Die Jüdin von Toledo"

Translated by
George Henry Danton and Annina Periam Danton
(1914)

Editor (2009): Andrew Moore

Cover photo: "Franz Grillparzer"
(Source: The German Classics.
German Publication Society, New York, 1914)

ISBN 978-1-59569-139-2
Library of Congress Control Number: 2009934401

www.mondialbooks.com

The Jewess of Toledo (1851) may perhaps be said to mark the climax of Grillparzer's productive activity. It is an eminently modern drama of passion in classical dignity of form. Grillparzer noted the subject as early as 1813. In 1824 he read Lope de Vega's play on it, and wrote in trochees two scenes of his own; in 1848-49 — perhaps with Lola Montez and the king of Bavaria in mind — he worked further on it, and about 1855 brought the work to an end. The play is properly called *The Jewess of Toledo;* for Rachel, the Jewess, is at the centre of the action, and is a marvelous creation — "a mere woman, nothing but her sex"; but the king, though relatively passive, is the most important character. He is attracted to Rachel by a charm that he has never known in his coldly virtuous English consort, and, after an error forgivable because made comprehensible, is taught the duty of personal sacrifice to morality and to the state. In doctrine and in inner form this drama is comparable to Hebbel's *Agnes Bernauer;* it is a companion piece to *A Faithful Servant of his Master*,* and the sensuality of Rachel contrasts instructively with the spirituality of Hero**. The genuine dramatic collision of antithetical forces produces, furthermore, a new synthesis, the effect of which is to make us wish morality less austere and the sense of obligation stronger than they at first are in two persons good by nature but caused to err by circumstances.

---

* *Ein treuer Diener seines Herrn;* drama by Franz Grillparzer, 1830.

** Hero in: *Des Meeres und der Liebe Wellen;* drama by Franz Grillparzer, 1829.

The drama was for Grillparzer what Goethe said it should always be, a present reality; and for the greater impressiveness of this reality he is fond of the use of visible objects — whether they be symbols, like the Golden Fleece in *Medea**, the lyre in *Sappho***, the medallion in *The Jewess of Toledo,* or characteristic weapons, accoutrement, and apparel. Everything expressive is welcome to him, gesture or inarticulate sound reinforces the spoken word or replaces it. Unusually sensuous language and comparative fulness of sententious passages go hand in hand with a laconic habit which indulges in many ellipses and is content to leave to the actor the task of making a single word convey the meaning of a sentence.

Grillparzer's plays were written for the stage. He abhorred what the Germans call a book drama, and had, on the other hand, the highest respect for the judgment of a popular audience as to the fact whether a play were fit for the stage or not. The popular audience was a jury from which there was no appeal on this question of fact.

William Guild Howard
(1914)

---

* *Medea;* third part of the drama *Das goldene Vlies* by Franz Grillparzer, 1819.

** *Sappho;* drama by Franz Grillparzer, 1818.

DRAMATIS PERSONÆ

ALFONSO VIII., *the Noble, King of Castile.*

ELEANOR OF ENGLAND, *Daughter of Henry II., his Wife.*

THE PRINCE, *their Son.*

MANRIQUE, *Count of Lara, Governor of Castile.*

DON GARCERAN, *his Son.*

DOÑA CLARA, *Lady in Waiting to the Queen.*

The Queen's Waiting Maid.

ISAAC, *the Jew.*

ESTHER, *his Daughter.*

RACHEL, *his Daughter.*

REINERO, *the King's Page.*

*Nobles, Court Ladies, Petitioners, Servants,
and Other People.*

Place: *Toledo and Vicinity.*
Time: *about 1195 A.D.*

ACT I

In the Royal Garden at Toledo.
Enter Isaac, Rachel, and Esther.

ISAAC. Back, go back, and leave the garden!
Know ye not it is forbidden?
When the King here takes his pleasure
Dares no Jew — ah, God will damn them!
Dares no Jew to tread the earth here!

RACHEL *(singing)*. La-la-la-la.

ISAAC.   Don't you hear me?

RACHEL. Yes, I hear thee.

ISAAC.   Hear, and linger?

RACHEL. Hear, yet linger!

ISAAC. Oh, Oh, Oh! Why doth God try me?
To the poor I've given my portion,
I have prayed and I have fasted,
Unclean things I've never tasted:
Nay! And yet God tries me thus.

RACHEL *(to Esther)*.
Ow! Why dost thou pull my arm so?
I *will* stay, I am not going.
I just wish to see the King and
All the court and all their doings,
All their gold and all their jewels.
He is young, they say, and handsome,
White and red, I want to see him.

ISAAC. And suppose the servants catch thee?

RACHEL. Then I'll beg until they free me!

ISAAC. Yes, just like thy mother, eh?
She, too, looked at handsome Christians,
Sighed, too, for Egyptian flesh-pots;
Had I not so closely watched her
I should deem — well, God forgive me! —
That thy madness came that way,
Heritage of mean, base Christians;
Ah! I praise my first wife, noble!
                    (To Esther.)
Praise thy mother, good like thee,
Though not wealthy. Of the second
Did the riches aught avail me?
Nay, she spent them as she pleasured,
Now for feasts and now for banquets,
Now for finery and jewels.
Look! This is indeed her daughter!
Has she not bedeckt herself,
Shines she not in fine apparel
Like a Babel in her pride?

RACHEL *(singing)*. Am I not lovely,
                    Am I not rich?
See their vexation,
                    And I don't care — la, la, la, la.

ISAAC. There she goes with handsome shoes on;
Wears them out — what does it matter?
Every step costs me a farthing!
Richest jewels are her earrings,
If a thief comes, he will take them,
If they're lost, who'll find them ever?

RACHEL *(taking off an earring)*.
Lo! I take them off and hold them,

3

How they shine and how they shimmer!
Yet how little I regard them,
Haply, I to thee present them
(to Esther.)
Or I throw them in the bushes.

[She makes a motion as if throwing it away.]

ISAAC *(running in the direction of the throw).*
Woe, ah woe! Where did they go to?
Woe, ah woe! How find them ever?

ESTHER. These fine jewels? What can ail thee?

RACHEL. Dost believe me, then, so foolish
As to throw away possessions?
See, I have it in my hand here,
Hang it in my ear again and
On my cheek it rests in contrast.

ISAAC. Woe! Lost!

RACHEL.   Father come, I prithee!
See! the jewel is recovered.
I was jesting.

ISAAC.   Then may God —
Thus to tease me! And now, come!

RACHEL. Anything but this I'll grant thee.
I must see his Royal Highness,
And he me, too, yes, yes, me, too.
If he comes and if he asks them,
"Who is she, that lovely Jewess?"
"Say, how hight you?" — "Rachel, sire!
Isaac's Rachel! " I shall answer.
Then he'll pinch my cheek so softly.

Beauteous Rachel then they'll call me.
What if envy bursts to hear it,
Shall I worry if it vexes?

ESTHER. Father!

ISAAC.   What?

ESTHER.   The court approaches.

ISAAC. Lord of life, what's going to happen?
'Tis the tribe of Rehoboam.
Wilt thou go?

RACHEL.   Oh, father, listen!

ISAAC. Well then stay! But come thou, Esther,
Leave the fool here to her folly.
Let him touch her, let him kill her,
She herself hath idly willed it.
Esther, come!

RACHEL.   Oh, father, tarry!

ISAAC. Hasten, hasten; come, then, Esther!

[Exit with Esther.]

RACHEL. Not alone will I remain here!
Listen! Stay! Alas, they leave me.
Not alone will I remain here.
Ah! they come—Oh, sister, father!

[She hastens after them.]

Enter the King, the Queen, Manrique de Lara and suite.

KING *(entering)*. Allow the folk to stay!
   It harms me not;
For he who calleth me a King denotes

As highest among many me, and so
The people is a part of my own self.
(Turning to the Queen.)
And thou, no meager portion of myself,
Art welcome here in this my ancient home,
Art welcome in Toledo's faithful walls.
Gaze all about thee, let thy heart beat high,
For, know! thou standest at my spirit's fount.
There is no square, no house, no stone, no tree,
That is not witness of my childhood lot.
An orphan child, I fled my uncle's wrath,
Bereft of mother first, then fatherless,
Through hostile land — it was my own — I fled.
The brave Castilians me from place to place,
Like shelterers of villainy did lead,
And hid me from my uncle of Leon,
Since death did threaten host as well as guest.
But everywhere they tracked me up and down.
Then Estevan Illan, a don who long
Hath slept beneath the greensward of the grave,
And this man here, Manrique Lara, led me
To this, the stronghold of the enemy,
And hid me in the tower of St. Roman,
Which there you see high o'er Toledo's roofs.
There lay I still, but they began to strew
The seed of rumor in the civic ear,
And on Ascension Day, when all the folk
Was gathered at the gate of yonder fane,
They led me to the tower-balcony
And showed me to the people, calling down,
"Here in your midst, among you, is your King,
The heir of ancient princes; of their rights
And of your rights the willing guardian."

I was a child and wept then, as they said.
But still I hear it—ever that wild cry,
A single word from thousand bearded throats,
A thousand swords as in a single hand,
The people's hand.
                            But God the vict'ry gave,
The Leonese did flee; and on and on,
A standard rather than a warrior,
I with my army compassed all the land,
And won my vict'ries with my baby smile.
These taught and nurtured me with loving care,
And mother's milk flowed from their wounds
    for me.
And so, while other princes call themselves
The fathers of their people, I am son,
For what I am, I owe their loyalty.

MANRIQUE. If all that now thou art, most noble Sire,
Should really, as thou sayest, spring from thence,
Then gladly we accept the thanks, rejoice
If these our teachings and our nurture, thus
Are mirrored in thy fame and in thy deeds,
Then we and thou are equally in debt.
(To the Queen.)
Pray gaze on him with these thy gracious eyes;
Howe'er so many kings have ruled in Spain,
Not one compares with him in nobleness.
Old age, in truth, is all too wont to blame,
And I am old and cavil much and oft;
And when confuted in the council-hall
I secret wrath have ofttimes nursed—not long,
Forsooth—that royal word should weigh so much;
And sought some evil witness 'gainst my King,
And gladly had I harmed his good repute.

But always I returned in deepest shame —
The envy mine, and his the spotlessness.

KING. A teacher, Lara, and a flatt'rer, too?
But we will not dispute you this and that;
If I'm not evil, better, then, for you,
Although the man, I fear me, void of wrong,
Were also void of excellence as well;
For as the tree with sun-despising roots,
Sucks up its murky nurture from the earth,
So draws the trunk called wisdom, which indeed
Belongs to heaven itself in towering branch,
Its strength and being from the murky soil
Of our mortality — allied to sin.
Was ever a just man who ne'er was hard?
And who is mild, is oft not strong enough.
The brave become too venturesome in war.
What we call virtue is but conquered sin,
And where no struggle was, there is no power.
But as for me, no time was given to err,
A child — the helm upon my puny head,
A youth — with lance, high on my steed I sat,
My eye turned ever to some threat'ning foe,
Unmindful of the joys and sweets of life,
And far and strange lay all that charms and lures.
That there are women, first I learned to know
When in the church my wife was given me,
She, truly faultless if a human is,
And whom, I frankly say, I'd warmer love
If sometimes need to pardon were, not praise.
(To the Queen.)
Nay, nay, fear not, I said it but in jest!
The outcome we must all await — nor paint
The devil on the wall, lest he appear.

But now, what little respite we may have,
Let us not waste in idle argument.
The feuds within our land are stilled, although
They say the Moor will soon renew the fight,
And hopes from Africa his kinsman's aid,
Ben Jussuf and his army, bred in strife.
And war renewed will bring distress anew.
Till then we'll open this our breast to peace,
And take deep breath of unaccustomed joy.
Is there no news? — But did I then forget?
You do not look about you, Leonore,
To see what we have done to please you here.

QUEEN.   What ought I see?

KING.   Alas, O Almirante!
We have not hit upon it, though we tried.
For days, for weeks, we dig and dig and dig,
And hope that we could so transform this spot,
This orange-bearing, shaded garden grove,
To have it seem like such as England loves,
The austere country of my austere wife.
And she but smiles and smiling says me nay!
Thus are they all, Britannia's children, all;
If any custom is not quite their own,
They stare, and smile, and will have none of it;
Th' intention, Leonore, was good, at least,
So give these worthy men a word of thanks;
God knows how long they may have toiled for us.

QUEEN.   I thank you, noble sirs.

KING.   To something else!
The day has started wrong. I hoped to show
You houses, meadows, in the English taste,
Through which we tried to make this garden please;

We missed our aim. Dissemble not, O love!
'Tis so, and let us think of it no more.
To duty we devote what time remains,
Ere Spanish wine spice high our Spanish fare.
What, from the boundary still no messenger?
Toledo did we choose, with wise intent,
To be at hand for tidings of the foe.
And still there are none?

MANRIQUE.   Sire —

KING.   What is it, pray?

MANRIQUE. A messenger —

KING.   Has come? What then?

MANRIQUE *(pointing to the Queen).*

                              Not now.

KING. My wife is used to council and to war,
The Queen in everything shares with the King.

MANRIQUE. The messenger himself, perhaps, more
    than
The message —

KING.   Well, who is't?

MANRIQUE.   It is my son.

KING. Ah, Garceran! Pray let him come.
(To the Queen.)

                              Stay thou!
The youth, indeed, most grossly erred, when he
Disguised, slipped in the kemenate to spy
Upon the darling of his heart — Do not,
O Doña Clara, bow your head in shame,
The man is brave, although both young and rash,

My comrade from my early boyhood days;
And now implacability were worse
Than frivolous condoning of the fault.
And penance, too, methinks, he's done enough
For months an exile on our kingdom's bounds.

[At a nod from the Queen, one of the ladies of her suite withdraws.]

And yet she goes: O Modesty
More chaste than chastity itself!

Enter Garceran.

My friend,
What of the border? Are they all out there
So shy with maiden-modesty as you?
Then poorly guarded is our realm indeed!

GARCERAN. A doughty soldier, Sire, ne'er fears a foe,
But noble women's righteous wrath is hard.

KING. 'Tis true of righteous wrath!
   And do not think
That I with custom and propriety
Am less severe and serious than my wife,
Yet anger has its limits, like all else.
And so, once more, my Garceran, what cheer?
Gives you the foe concern in spite of peace?

GARCERAN. With bloody wounds, O Sire, as if in play,
On this side of the boundary and that
We fought, yet ever peace resembled war
So to a hair, that perfidy alone
Made all the difference. But now the foe
A short time holdeth peace.

KING.   'Tis bad!

GARCERAN.   We think
So too, and that he plans a mightier blow.
And rumor hath it that his ships convey
From Africa to Cadiz men and food,
Where secretly a mighty army forms,
Which Jussuf, ruler of Morocco, soon
Will join with forces gathered over seas;
And then the threat'ning blow will fall on us.

KING. Well, if they strike, we must return the blow.
A king leads them, and so a king leads you.
If there's a God, such as we know there is,
And justice be the utt'rance of his tongue,
I hope to win, God with us, and the right!
I grieve but for the peasants' bitter need,
Myself, as highest, should the heaviest bear.
Let all the people to the churches come
And pray unto the God of victory.
Let all the sacred relics be exposed,
And let each pray, who goeth to the fight.

GARCERAN. Without thy proclamation, this is done,
The bells sound far through all the borderland,
And in the temples gathereth the folk;
Only, alas, its zeal, erring as oft,
Expends itself on those of other faith,
Whom trade and gain have scattered through
    the land.
Mistreated have they here and there a Jew.

KING. And ye, ye suffer this? Now, by the Lord,
I will protect each one who trusts in me.
Their faith is their affair, their conduct mine.

GARCERAN. 'Tis said they're spies and hirelings of
the Moors.

KING. Be sure, no one betrays more than he knows,
And since I always have despised their gold,
I never yet have asked for their advice.
Not Christian and not Jew knows what shall be,
But I alone. Hence, by your heads, I urge —

[A woman's voice without.]
Woe, woe!

KING.   What is't?

GARCERAN.   An old man, Sire, is there,
A Jew, methinks, pursued by garden churls,
Two maidens with him, one of them, behold,
Is fleeing hither.

KING.   Good! Protection's here,
And thunder strike who harms one hair of hers.
(Calling behind the scenes.)
Hither, here I say!

RACHEL *comes in flight*

RACHEL.   They're killing me!
My father, too! Oh! is there none to help?

[She sees the Queen and kneels before her.]

Sublime one, shelter me from these. Stretch out
Thy hand and hold it over me, thy maid,
Not Jewess I to serve thee then, but slave.

*[She tries to take the hand of the Queen who turns
away.]*

13

RACHEL *(rising)*. Here, too, no safety? Terror
  everywhere?
Where shall I flee to? Here there stands a man
Whose moonbeam glances flood the soul with peace,
And everything about him proves him King.
Thou canst protect me, Sire, and oh, thou wilt!
I *will* not die, I *will* not, no, no, no!

*[She throws herself on the ground before the King and
seizes his right foot, bending her head to the ground.]*

KING *(to several who approach)*.

Let be!
Her senses have ta'en flight through fear,
And as she shudders, makes me tremble, too.

RACHEL *(sits up)*. And everything I have, *(taking off
  her bracelet)* this bracelet here,
This necklace and this costly piece of cloth,
(taking a shawl-like cloth from her neck)
It cost my father well-nigh forty pounds,
Real Indian stuff, I'll give that too — if you
Will leave me but my life: I will not die!

[She sinks back to her former position.]

Isaac and Esther are led in.

KING. What crime has he committed?

MANRIQUE.   Sire, thou know'st,
The entrance to the royal gardens is
Denied this people when the court is here.

KING. And I permit it, if it is forbidden.

ESTHER. He is no spy, O Sire, a merchant he,
In Hebrew are the letters that he bears,
Not in the Moorish tongue, not Arabic.

KING. 'Tis well, I doubt it not.
(Pointing to Rachel.)

And she?

ESTHER. My sister!

KING. Take her and carry her away.

RACHEL *(as Esther approaches her).* No, no!
They're seizing me, they're leading me away
To kill me!
(Pointing to her discarded finery.)
See, my ransom. Here will I
Remain a while and take a little sleep.
(Laying her cheek against the King's knee.)
Here safety is; and here 'tis good to rest.

QUEEN. Will you not go?

KING. You see that I am caught.

QUEEN. If you are caught, I still am free, I go!

[Exit with her women.]

KING. And now that, too! That which they would
prevent
They bring to pass with their false chastity.
(Sternly to Rachel.)
Arise, I tell thee—Give her back her shawl,
And let her go.

RACHEL. O, Sire, a little while.
My limbs are lamed,—I cannot, cannot walk.

*[She props her elbow on her knee and rests her head in
her hand.]*

KING *(stepping back).* And is she ever thus, so
timorous?

ESTHER.   Nay, for, a while ago, presumptuous,
In spite of us, she wished to see thee, Sire.

KING.   Me? She has paid it dear.

ESTHER.   At home, as well,
She plays her pranks, and jokes with man or dog,
And makes us laugh, however grave we be.

KING.   I would, indeed, she were a Christian, then,
And here at court, where things are dull enough:
A little fun might stand us in good stead.
Ho, Garceran!

GARCERAN.   Illustrious Sire and King!

ESTHER *(busy with Rachel).*   Stand up!
Stand up!

RACHEL   *(rising and taking off Esther's necklace, which
she adds to the other jewels).*
                And give, too, what *thou* hast,
It is my ransom.

ESTHER.   Well, so be it then.

KING.   What think you of all this?

GARCERAN.   What *I* think, Sire?

KING.   Dissemble not!   You are a connoisseur,
Myself have never looked at women much,
But *she* seems beautiful.

GARCERAN.   She is, O Sire!

KING.   Be strong then, for you shall accomp'ny her.

RACHEL *(who stands in the middle of the stage with
trembling knees and bent head, pushing up her sleeve).*
Put on my bracelet. Oh you hurt me so.

The necklace, too — indeed, that still hangs here.
The kerchief keep, I feel so hot and choked.

KING. Convey her home!

GARCERAN.   But, Sire, I fear —

KING.   Well, what?

GARCERAN. The people are aroused.

KING.   Ay, you are right.
Although a royal word protection is,
'Tis better that we give no cause to wrong.

ESTHER *(fixing Rachel's dress at the neck).*
Thy dress is all disturbed and all awry.

KING. Take her at first to one of those kiosks
There scattered through the garden, and at eve —

GARCERAN. I hear, my liege!

KING.   What was I saying? Oh!
Are you not ready yet?

ESTHER.   We are, my lord.

KING. At evening when the people all have gone,
Then lead her home and that will make an end.

GARCERAN. Come, lovely heathen!

KING.   Heathen? Stuff and nonsense!

ESTHER *(to Rachel, who prepares to go).*
And thankst thou not the King for so much grace?

RACHEL *(still exhausted, turning to the King).*
My thanks, O Sire, for all thy mighty care!
O were I not a poor and wretched thing —
(with a motion of her hand across her neck)
That this my neck, made short by hangman's hand,

17

That this my breast, a shield against thy foe —
But that thou wishest not!

KING.   A charming shield!
Now go, and God be with you. — Garceran,
(more softly)
I do not wish that she, whom I protect
Should be insulted by improper jests,
Or any way disturbed —

RACHEL *(with her hand on her brow)*. I cannot walk.

KING *(as Garceran is about to offer his arm)*.
And why your arm? The woman can assist.
And do thou, gaffer, watch thy daughter well,
The world is ill! Do thou protect thy hoard.

[Exeunt Rachel and her kin, led by Garceran.]

KING *(watching them)*. She totters still in walking.
  All her soul
A sea of fear in e'er-renewing waves.
(Putting down his foot)
She held my foot so tightly in her grasp,
It almost pains me. Strange it is, a man
When cowardly, with justice is despised —
A woman shows her strength when she is weak.
Ah, Almirante, what say *you* to this?

MANRIQUE. I think, the punishment you gave my son,
Is, noble Sire, both subtle and severe.

KING. The punishment?

MANRIQUE.   To guard this common trash.

KING. Methinks the punishment is not so hard.
Myself have never toyed with women much,
(Pointing to his suite.)

18

But these, perchance, think otherwise than you.
But now, avaunt all pictures so confused!
And dine we, for my body needs new strength,
And with the first glad draught this festal day,
Let each one think — of what he wants to think.
No ceremony! Forward! Hasten! On!

*[As the court arranges itself on both sides and the King
goes through the centre, the curtain falls.]*

ACT II

*A drop scene showing part of the garden. At the right,
a garden-house with a balcony and a door, to which
several steps lead up.*

Garceran enters through the door.

GARCERAN. And so before I'm caught, I'll save myself!
The girl is beautiful, and is a fool;
But love is folly; wherefore such a fool
Is more to fear than e'er the slyest was.
Besides, 'tis necessary that I bring,
While still there's time, my good repute again
To honor, and my love for Doña Clara,
Most silent she of all that never talk;
The wise man counts escape a victory.

A page of the King enters.

PAGE. Sir Garceran—

GARCERAN.   Ah, Robert, what's a-foot?

PAGE. The King, my lord, commanded me to see
If still you were with her entrusted you—

GARCERAN. If I am here? Why, he commanded—
    friend!
You were to see were I, perhaps, upstairs?
Just tell him that the girl is in the house,
And I outside. That answer will suffice.

PAGE. The King himself!

GARCERAN.   Your majesty!

[The King comes wrapped in a cloak. Exit Page.]

KING.   Well, friend!
Still here?

GARCERAN. Why, did you not yourself command
That only with the evening's first approach —

KING. Yes, yes, but now on second thought it seems
Far better that you travel while 'tis day —
They say thou'rt brave.

GARCERAN.   So you believe, O Sire —

KING. Methinks thou honorest the royal word
Which would unharmed know what it protects.
But custom is the master of mankind;
Our wills will often only what they must.
And so, depart. But tell me, what doth she!

GARCERAN. At first, there was a weeping without end,
But time brings comfort, as the saying is;
And so 'twas here. Soon cheerfulness, yea jest,
Had banished all her former abject fear;
Then there was pleasure in the shining toys,
And wonder at the satin tapestries.
We measured every curtained stuff by yards,
Till now we've settled down and feel at home.

KING. And does she seem desirous to return?

GARCERAN. It sometimes seems she does, and then
    does not.
A shallow mind ne'er worries for the morrow.

KING. Of course thou didst not hesitate to throw
To her the bait of words, as is thy wont?
How did she take it, pray?

GARCERAN.   Not badly, Sire.

KING. Thou liest! But in truth thou'rt lucky, boy!
And hover'st like a bird in cheerful skies,
And swoopest down wherever berries lure,
And canst adjust thyself at the first glance.
I am a King; my very word brings fear.
Yet I, were I the first time in my life
To stand in woman's presence, fear should know!
How dost begin? Pray, teach me what to do;
I am a novice in such arts as these,
And nothing better than a grown-up child.
Dost sigh?

GARCERAN.   Oh, Sire, how sadly out of date!

KING.   Well then, dost gaze? Does then Squire
  Gander gawk
Till Lady Goose-quill gawks again? Is't so? And
next, I ween, thou takest up thy lute,
And turning towards the balcony, as here,
Thou singst a croaking song, to which the moon,
A yellow pander, sparkles through the trees;
The flowers sweet intoxicate the sense,
Till now the proper opportunity
Arrives — the father, brother — spouse, perhaps —
Has left the house on similar errand bent.
And now the handmaid calls you gently: "Pst!"
You enter in, and then a soft, warm hand
Takes hold of yours and leads you through the halls,
Which, endless as the gloomy grave, spur on
The heightened wish, until, at last, the musk,
The softened lights that come through curtains' folds,
Do tell you that your charming goal is reached.
The door is ope'd, and bright, in candle gleam,
On velvet dark, with limbs all loosed in love,

Her snow-white arm enwrapped in ropes of pearls,
Your darling leans with gently drooping head,
The golden locks—no, no, I say they're black—
Her raven locks—and so on to the end!
Thou seest, Garceran, I learn right well,
And Christian, Mooress, Jewess, 'tis the same.

GARCERAN. We frontier warriors prize, for lack of
  choice,
Fair Moorish women, but the Jewess, Sire,—

KING. Pretend thou not to pick and choose thy fare!
I wager, if the maiden there above
Had given thee but a glance, thou'dst be aflame.
I love it not, this folk, and yet I know
That what disfigures it, is our own work;
We lame them, and are angry when they limp,
And yet, withal, this wandering shepherd race
Has something great about it, Garceran.
We are today's, we others; but their line
Runs from Creation's cradle, where our God,
In human form, still walked in Paradise,
And cherubim were guests of patriarchs,
And God alone was judge, and was the law.
Within this fairy world there is the truth
Of Cain and Abel, of Rebecca's craft,
Of Rachel, who by Jacob's service wooed—
How hight this maiden?

GARCERAN.   Sire, I know not.

KING.   Oh!
Of great King Ahasuerus, who his hand
Stretched out o'er Esther; she, though Jewess, was
His wife, and, like a god, preserved her race.

23

Christian and Moslem both their lineage trace
Back to this folk, as oldest and as first;
Thus they have doubts of us, not we of them.
And though, like Esau, it has sold its right,
We ten times daily crucify our God
By grievous sins and by our vile misdeeds —
The Jews have crucified him only once!
Now let us go! Or, rather, stay thou here;
Conduct her hence, and mark well where she lives.
Perhaps some time, when worn by weary cares,
I'll visit her, and there enjoy her thanks.
(About to go, he hears a noise in the house and stops.)
What is't?

GARCERAN. Confusion in the house; it seems
Almost as if they bring thy praise to naught;
Among themselves they quarrel —

KING *(going to the house).* What about?

Isaac comes from the garden-house.

ISAAC *(speaking back into the house).*
Stay then, and risk your heads, if so ye will,
You've nearly lost them once. I'll save myself.

KING. Ask what he means.

GARCERAN. My good man, tell, how now?

ISAAC *(to Garceran).*
Ah, Sir, it is then you, our guardian!
My little Rachel speaks of you so oft;
She likes you.

KING. To the point. What babbling this —

ISAAC. Who is this lord?

GARCERAN.   It makes no difference. Speak!
What is the cause of all that noise above?

ISAAC *(speaking up to the window).*
Look out, you're going to catch it—now look out!
(To Garceran.)
Yourself have seen my little Rachel-girl,
And how she wept and groaned and beat her breasts,
As if half crazed. Of course you have, my life!—
She hardly knew the danger had been passed
When back again her old high spirits came;
She laughed, and danced, and sang; half mad again
She shoved awry the sacred furniture
By dead men watched, and raves—as now you hear.
Hangs from her girdle not a chatelaine?
Her keys she tries in every closet lock,
And opens all the doors along the wall.
There hang within all sorts of things to wear,
And angels, devils, beggars vie with kings
In gay attire—

KING *(aside to Garceran).* Our carnival costumes.

ISAAC. She chose, herself, a plumed crown from
    these,—
It was not gold, but only gilded tin—
One tells it by the weight, worth twenty pence;
About her shoulders throws a trained robe
And says she is the queen—
(Speaking back.) Oh yes, thou fool!
Then in the ante-chamber next, there hangs
A picture of the King, whom God preserve!
She takes it from the wall, bears it about,
Calling it husband with endearing words,
And holds it to her breast.

[King goes hastily toward the garden house.]

GARCERAN.   Oh, mighty Sire!

ISAAC *(stepping back).*   Alas!

KING *(standing on the steps, quietly).*
That game is worth a nearer look.
What's more, 'twill soon be time for you to go;
You should not miss the favorable hour.
But you, old man, must come. For not alone,
Nor unobserved would I approach your children.

[Goes into the house.]

ISAAC. Was that the King? Oh, woe!

GARCERAN.   Proceed within.

ISAAC. If he should draw his sword, we all are
   doomed!

GARCERAN. Go in. And as for being afraid, 'tis not
For you nor for your daughter that I fear.

*[He pushes the hesitating Isaac into the garden house
and follows him.]*

*Room in the pavilion. In the background to the left
a door; in the foreground to the right, another door.
Rachel, with a plumed crown on her head and gold
embroidered mantle about her shoulders, is trying
to drag an armchair from the neighboring room, on
the right. Esther has come in through the principal
entrance.*

RACHEL. The armchair should stand here, here in
   the middle.

ESTHER. For Heaven's sake, O Rachel, pray look out;
Your madness else will bring us all to grief.

RACHEL. The King has given this vacant house to us;
As long as we inhabit it, it's ours.

[They have dragged the chair to the centre.]

RACHEL *(looking at herself).*
Now don't you think my train becomes me well?
And when I nod, these feathers also nod.
I need just one thing more—I'll get it—wait!

[Goes back through the side door.]

ESTHER. Oh, were we only far from here, at home!
My father, too, comes not, whom she drove off.

RACHEL *(comes back with an unframed picture).*
The royal image taken from its frame
I'll bear it with me.

ESTHER.   Art thou mad again?
How often I have warned thee!

RACHEL.   Did I heed?

ESTHER. By Heaven, no!

RACHEL.   Nor will I heed you now.
The picture pleases me. Just see how fine!
I'll hang it in my room, close by my bed.
At morn and eventide I'll gaze at it,
And think such thoughts as one may think when one
Has shaken off the burden of one's clothes
And feels quite free from every onerous weight.
But lest they think that I have stolen it—
I who am rich—what need have I to steal?—
My portrait which you wear about your neck
We'll hang up where the other used to be.
Thus he may look at mine, as I at his,
And think of me, if he perchance forgot.

27

The footstool bring me hither; I am Queen,
And I shall fasten to the chair this King.
They say that witches who compel to love
Stick needles, thus, in images of wax,
And every prick goes to a human heart
To hinder or to quicken life that's real.

[She fastens the picture by the four corners to the back of the chair.]

Oh, would that blood could flow with every prick,
That I could drink it with my thirsty lips,
And take my pleasure in the ill I'd done!
It hangs there, no less beautiful than dumb.
But I will speak to it as were I Queen,
With crown and mantle which become me well.

[She has seated herself on the footstool before the picture.]

Oh, hypocrite, pretending piety,
Full well I know your each and every wile!
The Jewess struck your fancy — don't deny!
And, by my mighty word, she's beautiful,
And only with myself to be compared.

[The King, followed by Garceran and Isaac, has entered and placed himself behind the chair, and leans upon the back of the chair, watching her.]

(Rachel continues) But I, your Queen, I will not
    suffer it,
For know that I am jealous as a cat.
Your silence only makes your guilt seem more.
Confess! You liked her? Answer, yes!

KING.   Well, yes!

[Rachel starts, looks at the picture, then up, recognizes the King, and remains transfixed on the footstool.]

KING *(stepping forward).*
Art frightened? Thou hast willed it, and I say't.
Compose thyself, thou art in friendly hands!

[He stretches his hand toward her, she leaps from the stool and flees to the door at the right where she stands panting and with bowed head.]

KING. Is she so shy?

ESTHER. Not always, gracious Sire!
Not shy, but timid.

KING. Do I seem so grim?
(Approaching her. Rachel shakes her head violently.)
Well then, my dearest child, I pray be calm!
Yes, I repeat it, thou hast pleased me well;
When from this Holy War I home return
To which my honor and my duty call,
Then in Toledo I may ask for thee —
Where dwell you in this city?

ISAAC *(quickly).* Jew Street, Sire —
Ben Mathes' house.

ESTHER, If not, before you come,
We're driven out.

KING. My word! That shall not be.
And I can keep a promise to protect.
So if at home you are as talkative
And cheerful as I hear you erstwhile were —
Not shy, as now, I'll pass the time away,
And draw a breath far from the fogs of court.
But now depart; the time has long since come.

Go with them, Garceran; but, ere you go,
My picture now return to where it was.

RACHEL *(rushing to the chair).* The picture's mine!

KING.   What ails thee, child? It must
Go back into the frame where it belongs.

RACHEL *(to Garceran).*
The picture touch not, nor the pins therein,
Or I shall fix it with a deeper thrust—
(Making a motion toward the picture with a pin.)
Behold, right in the heart!

KING.   By Heaven, stop!
Thou almost frightenedst me. Who art thou, girl?
Art mistress of the black and criminal arts,
That I should feel in my own breast the thrust
Thou aimèdst at the picture?

ESTHER.   Noble Sire,
She's but a spoiled child, and a wanton girl, ·
And has no knowledge of forbidden arts!
It happened to occur to her—that's all!

KING. One ought not boldly play with things like
    these.
It drove my blood up to my very eyes,
And still I see the world all in a haze.
(To Garceran.)
Is she not beautiful?

GARCERAN.   She is, my lord.

KING. See how the waves of light glow o'er her
form!

*[Rachel has meanwhile taken off the picture and rolled
it up.]*

KING. Thou absolutely wilt not give it up?

RACHEL *(to Esther)*. I'll take it.

KING.   Well, then, in the name of God!
He will prevent that any ill befall.
But only go! Take, Garceran,
The road that down behind the garden leads.
The folk's aroused; it loves, because it's weak,
To test that weakness on some weaker one.

GARCERAN *(at the window)*.
Behold, O Sire, where comes th' entire court, —
The Queen herself leads on her retinue.

KING. Comes here? Accursed! Is here no other door?
Let not the prying crew find here false cause
To prattle!

GARCERAN *(pointing to the side door)*.
            Sire, this chamber.

KING.   Think you, then,
Before my servants I should hide myself?
And yet I fear the pain 'twould give the Queen;
She might believe — what I myself believe,
And so I save my troubled majesty.
See to it that she very soon depart.

[Exit into the side room.]

ESTHER. I told you so! It is misfortune's road.

Enter the Queen accompanied by Manrique de Lara and several others.

QUEEN. They told me that the King was in this place.

GARCERAN. He was, but went away.

QUEEN.   The Jewess here.

31

MANRIQUE. Arrayed like madness freed from every
  bond,
With all the tinsel-state of puppet-play!
Lay off the crown, for it befits thee not,
Even in jest; the mantle also doff!

[Esther has taken both off.]

What has she in her hand?

RACHEL.   It is my own.

MANRIQUE. But first we'll see!

ESTHER.   Nay, we are not so poor
That we should stretch our hands for others' goods!

MANRIQUE *(going toward the side door).*
And, too, in yonder chamber let us look,
If nothing missing, or perhaps if greed
With impudence itself as here, has joined.

GARCERAN *(barring the way).*
Here, father, call I halt!

MANRIQUE.   Know'st thou me not?

GARCERAN. Yes, and myself as well. But there be
  duties
Which even a father's rights do not outweigh.

MANRIQUE. Look in my eye! He cannot bear to do it!
Two sons I lose on this unhappy day.
(To the Queen.) Will you not go?

QUEEN.   I would, but cannot. Yes,

I surely can, by Heaven, for I must.
(To Garceran.)
Although your office an unknightly one,
I thank you that you do it faithfully;

'Twere death to see — but I can go and suffer —
If you should meet your master ere the eve,
Say, to Toledo I returned — alone.

[The Queen and her suite go out.]

GARCERAN. Woe worth the chance that chose this
    day of all,
To bring me home — from war to worse than war!

RACHEL *(to Esther, who is busied with her).*
And had my life been forfeit, I'd have stayed.

ESTHER *(to Garceran).*
I pray you now to bring us quickly home.

GARCERAN. First, let me ask the King his royal will.
(Knocking at the side door.)
Sire! What? No sign of life within? Perchance
An accident? Whate'er it be — I'll ope!

*[The King steps out and remains standing in the
foreground as the others withdraw to the back of the
stage.]*

KING. So honor and repute in this our world
Are not an even path on which the pace,
Simple and forward, shows the tendency,
The goal, our worth. They're like a juggler's rope,
On which a misstep plunges from the heights,
And every stumbling makes a butt for jest.
Must I, but yesterday all virtues' model,
Today shun every slave's inquiring glance?
Begone then, eager wish to please the mob,
Henceforth determine we ourselves our path!
(Turning to the others.)
What, you still here?

GARCERAN.   We wait your high command.

KING. If you had only always waited it,
And had remained upon the boundary!
Examples are contagious, Garceran.

GARCERAN. A righteous prince will punish every fault,
His own as well as others'; but, immune,
He's prone to vent his wrath on others' heads.

KING. Not such a one am I, my friend. Be calm!
We are as ever much inclined to thee;
And now, take these away, forever, too.
What's whim in others, is, in princes, sin.
(As he sees Rachel approaching.)
Let be! But first this picture lay aside,
And put it in the place from whence you took 't.
It is my will! Delay not!

RACHEL *(to Esther).*   Come thou, too.
(As both approach the side door).
Hast thou, as is thy wont, my picture on?

ESTHER. What wilt?

RACHEL.   My will — and should the worst betide —

[They go to the side door.]

KING. Then to the border, straight I'll follow thee;
And there we'll wash in Moorish blood away
The equal shame that we have shared this day,
That we may bear once more the gaze of men.

[The girls return.]

RACHEL. I did it.

KING.   Now away, without farewell!

ESTHER. Our thanks to thee, O Sire!

RACHEL.   Not mine, I say.

KING. So be it; thankless go!

RACHEL.   I'll save it up.

KING. That is, for never!

RACHEL.   I know better.
(To Esther.)

                                    Come.

[They go, accompanied by Garceran, Isaac bowing deeply.]

KING. And high time was it that she went; in sooth,
The boredom of a royal court at times
Makes recreation a necessity.
Although this girl has beauty and has charm
Yet seems she overbold and violent,
And one does well to watch what one begins.
Alonzo!

[Enter a servant.]

SERVANT.   Mighty Sire?

KING.   The horses fetch.

SERVANT. Toledo, Sire?

KING.   Nay, to Alarcos, friend.
We're for the border, for the war, and so
Make ready only what we need the most.
For in Toledo four eyes threaten me;
Two full of tears, the other two, of fire.
She would not leave my picture here behind,
And bade defiance unto death itself.
And yet there needed but my stern command
To make her put it back where it belonged.

35

She tried her actress arts on me, that's all;
But did she put it in the frame again?
Since I am leaving here for many moons
Let all be undisturbed as 'twas before;
Of this affair let every trace be gone.

*[He goes into the ante-chamber. A pause as one of the
servants takes up from the chair the clothes which
Rachel had worn, but holds the crown in his hand. The
King comes back holding Rachel's picture.]*

KING. My picture gone — and this one in its place!
It is her own, and burns within my hand —
(Throwing the picture on the floor.)
Avaunt! Avaunt! Can boldness go so far?
This may not be, for while I think of her
With just repugnance, this her painted image
Stirs up the burning passion in my breast.
Then, too, within her hands my picture rests!
They talk of magic, unallowed arts,
Which this folk practises with such-like things
And something as of magic o'er me comes —
(To the servant.)
Here, pick this up and spur thee on until
Thou overtake them.

SERVANT.   Whom, my liege?

KING.   Whom? Whom?
The girls of course, I mean, and Garceran;
Return this picture to the girls and ask —

SERVANT. What, Sire?

KING.   Shall my own servants then become
The sharers in the knowledge of my shame ?

I'll force th' exchange myself, if it must be!
Take up the picture — I will touch it not!

[The servant has picked up the picture.]

KING. HOW clumsy! Hide it in your breast; but nay,
If there, it would be warmed by other's glow!
Give 't here, myself will take it; follow me —
We'll overtake them yet! But I surmise,
Since now suspicion's rife, there may some harm,
Some accident befall them unawares.
My royal escort were the safest guide.
Thou, follow me!

[He has looked at the picture, then has put it in his bosom.]

     Stands there not, at the side,
The Castle Retiro, where, all concealed,
My forebear, Sancho, with a Moorish maid —?

SERVANT. Your Majesty, 'tis true!

KING.   We'll imitate
Our forebears in their bravery, their worth,
Not when they stumble in their weaker hours.
The task is, first of all to conquer self —
And then against the foreign conqueror!
Retiro hight the castle? — Let me see!
Oh yes, away! And be discreet! But then —
Thou knowest nothing! All the better. Come!

[Exit with servant.]

ACT III

Garden in the royal villa. In the background flows the
Tagus. A roomy arbor toward the front at the right. At
the left, several suppliants in a row, with petitions in
their hands. Isaac stands near them.

ISAAC. YOU were already told to linger not.
My daughter soon will come to take the air.
And *he* is with her — *he;* I say not who.
So tremble and depart, and your requests
Take to the King's advisers in Toledo.

[He takes the petition from one of them.]

Let's see! 'Twon't do.

PETITIONER.   You hold it upside down.

ISAAC. Because the whole request is topsy-turvy —
And you are, too. Disturb no more — depart.

2D PETIT. Sir Isaac, in Toledo me you knew.

ISAAC. I know you not. In these last days my eyes
Have suddenly grown very, very weak.

2D PETIT. But I know you! Here is the purse of gold
You lost, which I herewith restore to you.

ISAAC. The purse I lost? I recognize it! Yea,
'Twas greenish silk — with ten piasters in 't!

2D PETIT. Nay, twenty.

ISAAC.   Twenty? Well, my eye is good;
My mem'ry fails me, though, from time to time!

This sheet, no doubt, explains the circumstance —
Just where you found the purse, perhaps, and how.
There is no further need that this report
Should go on file. And yet, just let me have 't!
We will convey it to the proper place,
That every one may know your honesty!

*[The petitioners present their petitions; he takes one in
each hand and throws them to the ground.]*

No matter what it be, your answer's there.
(To a third.)
I see you have a ring upon your hand.
The stone is good, let's see!

[The suppliant hands over the ring.]

                         That flaw, of course,
Destroys its perfect water! Take it back.

[He puts the ring on his own finger.]

3D PETIT. You've put it on your own hand!

ISAAC.   What, on mine?
Why so I have! I thought I'd given it back.
It is so tight I cannot get it off.

3D PETIT. Keep it, but, pray, take my petition too.

ISAAC *(busy with the ring)*. I'll take them both in
  memory of you.
The King shall weigh the ring — I mean, of course,
Your words — although the flaw is evident —
The flaw that's in the stone — you understand.
Begone now, all of you! Have I no club?
Must I be bothered with this Christian pack?

[Garceran has meanwhile entered.]

GARCERAN. Good luck! I see you sitting in the reeds,
But find you're pitching high the pipes you cut.

ISAAC. The royal privacy's entrusted me;
The King's not here, he does not wish to be.
And who disturbs him — even you, my lord,
I must bid you begone! Those his commands.

GARCERAN. You sought a while ago to find a club;
And when you find it, bring it me. I think
Your back could use it better than your hand.

ISAAC. How you flare up! That is the way with
  Christians?
They're so direct of speech — but patient waiting,
And foresight, humble cleverness, they lack.
The King is pleased much to converse with me.

GARCERAN. When he is bored and flees his inner self,
E'en such a bore as you were less a bore.

ISAAC. He speaks to me of State and of finance.

GARCERAN. Are you, perhaps, the father of the new
Decree that makes a threepence worth but two?

ISAAC. Money, my friend, 's the root of everything.
The enemy is threat'ning — buy you arms!
The soldier, sure, is sold, and that for cash.
You eat and drink your money; what you eat
Is bought, and buying's money — nothing else.
The time will come when every human soul
Will be a sight-draft and a short one, too;
I'm councilor to the King, and if yourself
Would keep in harmony with Isaac's luck —

GARCERAN. In harmony with you? It is my curse
That chance and the accursed seeming so

Have mixed me in this wretched piece of folly,
Which to the utmost strains my loyalty.

ISAAC. My little Rachel daily mounts in grace!

GARCERAN. Would that the King, like many another
   one,
In jest and play had worn youth's wildness off!
But he, from childhood, knowing only men,
Brought up by men and tended but by men,
Nourished with wisdom's fruits before his time,
Taking his marriage as a thing of course,
The King now meets, the first time in his life,
A woman, female, nothing but her sex,
And she avenges on this prodigy
The folly of too staid, ascetic youth.
A noble woman's half, yes all, a man—
It is their faults that make them woman-kind.
And that resistance, which the oft deceived
Gains through experience, the King has not;
A light disport he takes for bitter earn'st.
But this shall not endure, I warrant thee!
The foe is at the borders, and the King
Shall hie him where long since he ought to be;
Myself shall lead him hence. And so an end.

ISAAC. Try what you can! And if not with us, then
You are against us, and will break your neck
In vain attempt to clear the wide abyss.
(The sound of flutes.)
But hark! With cymbals and with horns they come,
As Esther with King Ahasuerus came,
Who raised the Jews to fame and high estate.

GARCERAN. Must I, then, see in this my King's
   debauch

A picture of myself from early days,
And be ashamed for both of us at once?

[A boat upon which are the King, Rachel and suite,
appears on the river.]

KING. Lay to! Here is the place — the arbor here.
RACHEL. The skiff is rocking — hold me, lest I fall.

[The King has jumped to the shore.]

RACHEL. And must I walk to shore upon this board
So thin and weak?

KING.   Here, take my hand, I pray!

RACHEL. No, no, I'm dizzy.

GARCERAN *(to himself).*   Dizzy are you? Humph!

KING *(who has conducted her to the shore).*
It is accomplished now — this mighty task!

RACHEL. No, never will I enter more a ship.
(Taking the King's arm.)
Permit me, noble Sire, I am so weak!
Pray feel my heart, how fev'rishly it beats!

KING. To fear, is woman's right; but you abuse it.
RACHEL. You now, hard-hearted, take away your aid!
And, oh, these garden walks, how hard they are!
With stones, and not with sand, they're roughly
    strewn
For men to walk on, not for women's feet

KING. Put down a carpet, ye, that we have peace.

RACHEL. I feel it well — I merely burden you!
Oh, were my sister only here with me,
For I am sick and tired unto death!
Naught but these pillows here?

(Throwing the pillows in the arbor violently about.)
                                        No, no, no, no!

KING *(laughing).* I see your weakness happily abates.
(Catching sight of Garceran.)
Ah, Garceran! Behold, she's but a child!

GARCERAN. A spoiled child, surely!

KING.   Yes, they all are that.
It suits her well!

GARCERAN.   According to one's tastes!

KING. See, Garceran! I feel how wrong I am;
And yet I know there needeth but a nod,
A simple word, to make it all dissolve —
This dream — into the nothing that it is.
And so I suffer it because I've need,
In this confusion which myself have caused.
How is the army?

GARCERAN.   As you long have known,
The enemy is arming.

KING.   So shall we.
A few days more, and I shall put away
This toying from me, and forevermore;
Then time and counsel shall be found again.

GARCERAN. Mayhap the counsel, but the time slips
    by!

KING. With deeds we shall regain the ground that's
    lost.

RACHEL. I hear them speaking; and I know of what
— Of blood, of war, of heathen slaughter, too;
And that one there is plotting, too, 'gainst me.
He lures his master to the distant camp

43

And frees the pathway of my foes to me.
And yet, Sir Garceran, I like you well —
You know how one should treat with tender maids.
They tell me of your love's bold wooing, much,
Of deeds performed within the lists of love;
You are not like the King, your master, who,
When tenderest, is e'er a little rough,
Who straightway rues each loving word he's said,
And in whose love I feel a secret hate.
Come here, sit down by me, I wish to talk,
And not be lonesome in this concourse loud.
I see you come not. No, they hold you back

[Weeping.]

Not any comfort give they me, nor joy.
They hold me here, apart, in slavery.
Would I were home again in father's house,
Where every one is at my beck and call,
Instead of here, — the outcast of contempt.

KING. Go thou to her!

GARCERAN. What? Shall I?

KING. Go, I say!

RACHEL. Sit down by me, but nearer, nearer — so!
Once more I say, I love you, Garceran.
You are, indeed, a knight without a flaw,
Not merely knight in name, as they it learn —
Those iron, proud Castilians — from their foes,
The Moors. — But these Castilians imitate
In manner borrowed, therefore rough and crude,
What those, with delicate and clever art,
Are wont to practise as a native gift.
Give me your hand. Just see, how soft it is!

And yet you wield a sword as well as they.
But you're at home in boudoirs, too, and know
The pleasing manners of a gentler life.
From Doña Clara cometh not this ring?
She's far too pale for rosy-cheekèd love,
Were not the color which her face doth lack
Replaced by e'er renewing blush of shame.
But many other rings I see you have—
How many sweethearts have you? Come, confess!

GARCERAN. Suppose I ask the question now of you?

RACHEL. I've never loved. But I *could* love, if e'er
In any breast *that* madness I should find
Which could enthrall me, were my own heart
    touched.
Till then I follow custom's empty show,
Traditional in love's idolatry,
As in the fanes of stranger-creeds one kneels.

KING (*who meanwhile has been pacing up and down,
now stands in the foreground at the left and speaks in
an aside to a servant*).
Bring me my arms, and full accoutrements,
And wait for me beside the garden-house.
I will to camp where they have need of me.

[*Exit servant.*]

RACHEL. I beg you, see your King! He thinks he
    loves;
Yet when I speak to you and press your hand,
He worries not. With good economy,
He fills his garish day with business,
And posts his ledger, satisfied, at ev'n,
Out on you! You are all alike—you, too.

45

O were my sister here! She's wise — than I
Far cleverer! Yet, too, when in her breast
The spark of will and resolution falls,
She flashes out in flames, like unto mine.
Were she a man, she'd be a hero. Ye
Before her courage and her gaze should flinch.
Now let me sleep until she comes, for I
Myself am but the dreaming of a night.

[She lays her head on her arm and her arm on her pillows.]

GARCERAN *(steps to the King who stands watching the reclining Rachel)*. Most noble Sire —

KING *(still gazing)*.   Well?

GARCERAN.   May I now go back
Once more unto the army and the camp?

KING *(as above)*. The army left the camp? Pray tell
    me why.

GARCERAN. You hear me not — myself, *I* wish to go.

KING. And there you'll talk, with innuendo, prate —

GARCERAN. Of what?

KING.   Of me, of that which here took place.

GARCERAN. For that I'd need to understand it more.

KING. I see! Believest thou in sorcery?

GARCERAN. Since recently I almost do, my lord!

KING. And why is it but recently, I pray?

GARCERAN. Respect, I thought the wonted mate of
    love;
But love together with contempt, my lord —

KING. "Contempt" were far too hard a word; perhaps
An "unregard" — yet, nathless — marvelous!

GARCERAN. In sooth, the marvel is a little old,
For it began that day in Paradise
When God from Adam's rib created Eve.

KING. And yet he closed the breast when it was done,
And placed the will to guard the entering in.
Thou may'st to camp, but not alone: — with me.

RACHEL *(sitting up)*. The sun is creeping into my retreat.
Who props for me the curtain on yon side?
(Looking off stage at the right.)
There go two men, both bearing heavy arms;
The lance would serve my purpose very well.
(Calling off stage.)
Come here! This way! What, are ye deaf?
Come quick!

[The servant, returning with the lance and helmet, accompanied by a second servant bearing the King's shield and cuirass, enters.]

RACHEL. Give me your lance, good man, and stick the point
Here in the ground, and then the roof will be
Held up in that direction. Thus it throws
A broader shadow. Quickly, now! That's right!
You other fellow, like a snail, you bear
Your house upon your back, unless, perhaps,
A house for some one else. Show me the shield!
A mirror 'tis, in sooth! 'Tis crude, of course,
As all is, here, but in a pinch 'twill do.

(They hold the shield before her.)
One brings one's hair in order, pushes back
Whatever may have ventured all too far,
And praises God who made one passing fair.
This mirror's curve distorts me! Heaven help!
What puffy cheeks are these? No, no, my friend,
What roundness nature gives us, satisfies. —
And now the helmet — useless in a fight,
For it conceals what oft'nest wins — the eyes;
But quite adapted to the strife of love.
Put me the helm upon my head. — You hurt! —
And if one's love rebels and shows his pride,
Down with the visor!
(Letting it down.)
          He in darkness stands!
But should he dare, mayhap, to go from us,
And send for arms, to leave us here alone,
Then up the visor goes.
(She does it.)
          Let there be light!
The sun, victorious, drives away the fog.

KING *(going to her).* Thou silly, playing, wisely-
    foolish child!

RACHEL. Back, back! Give me the shield, give me
    the lance!
I am attacked, but can defend myself.

KING. Lay down thy arms! No ill approacheth thee!
(Taking both of her hands.)

Enter Esther from the left rear.

RACHEL. Ah thou, my little sister! Welcome, here!
Away with all this mummery, but quick!

Don't take my head off, too! How clumsy, ye!
(*Running to her.*)
Once more be welcome, O thou sister mine!
How I have long'd to have thee here with me!
And hast thou brought my bracelets and my jewels,
My ointments and my perfumes, with thee now,
As from Toledo's shops I ordered them?

ESTHER. I bring them and more weighty things
    besides —
Unwelcome news, a bitter ornament.
Most mighty Sire and Prince! The Queen has
    from
Toledo's walls withdrawn, and now remains
In yonder castle where ill-fortune first
Decreed that you and we should meet.
(*To Garceran.*)
                                        With her,
Your noble father, Don Manrique Lara,
Who summons all the kingdom's high grandees
From everywhere, in open letters, to
Discuss the common good, as if the land
Were masterless and you had died, O King.

KING. I think you dream!

ESTHER.   I am awake, indeed,
And must keep watch to save my sister's life.
They threaten her. She'll be the sacrifice!

RACHEL. O woe is me! Did I not long ago
Adjure you to return unto the court
And bring to naught the plotting of my foes? —
But you remain'd. Behold here are your arms,
The helm, the shield, and there the mighty spear ;
I'll gather them — but Oh, I cannot do't.

KING *(to* ESTHER*)*. Now tend the little girl. With
   every breath
She ten times contradicts what she has said.
I will to court; but there I need no arms;
With open breast, my hand without a sword,
I in my subjects' midst will boldly step
And ask: "Who is there here that dares rebel?"
They soon shall know their King is still alive
And that the sun dies not when evening comes,
But that the morning brings its rays anew.
Thou follow'st, Garceran!

GARCERAN.   I'm ready.

ESTHER.   What
Becomes of us?

RACHEL.   O stay, I beg you, stay!

KING. The castle's safe, the keeper faithful, too;
And he will guard you with his very life.
For though I feel that I have sinned full sore,
Let no one suffer who has trusted me
And who with me has shared my guilt and sin.
Come, Garceran! Or, rather, take the lead;
For if the estates were in assembly still,
Not called by me, nor rightfully convened,
I then must punish — much against my will.
Command them to disperse — and quickly, too!
Thy father tell: Although protector he
And regent for me in my boyhood days,
I now know how to guard my right myself —
Against him, too, against no matter whom.
Come on! And ye, farewell!

RACHEL *(approaching)*.   O mighty Prince!

KING. No more! I need my strength and steadfast
   will,
No parting words shall cripple my resolve.
Ye'll hear from me when I have done my work;
But how, and what the future brings, is still
Enwrapt in night and gloom. But come what may,
I give my princely word ye shall be safe.
Come, Garceran! With God! He be with you!

[Exeunt King and Garceran at the left.]

RACHEL. He loves me not—O, I have known it long!

ESTHER. O sister, useless is too tardy knowledge,
When injury has made us sadly wise.
I warned thee, but thou wouldst not ever heed.

RACHEL. He was so hot and ardent at the first!

ESTHER. And now makes up in coolness for his haste.

RACHEL. But I who trusted, what shall be my fate?
Come, let us flee!

ESTHER.   The streets are occupied;
Against us all the land is in revolt.

RACHEL. And so I then must die and am so young?
And I should like to live! Not live, indeed—
But die, unwarned, an unexpected death!
'Tis but the moment of our death that shocks!
(At Esther's neck.)
Unhappy am I, sister, hopeless, lost!
(After a pause, with a voice broken by sobs.)
And is the necklace set with amethysts,
Thou broughtst?

ESTHER.   It is. And pearls it has as bright
And many, too, as are thy tears.

RACHEL.   I would
Not look at it at all—at least not now.
But only if our prison lasts too long,
I'll try divert eternal wretchedness,
And shall adorn myself unto my death.
But see, who nears? Ha, ha, ha, ha, it is,
In sooth, our father, armèd cap-a-pie!

[Isaac, a helmet on his head, under his long coat a
cuirass, enters from the left.]

ISAAC. 'Tis I, the father of a wayward brood,
Who ere my time are shortening my days.
In harness, yes! When murder stalks abroad,
Will one's bare body save one from the steel?
A blow by chance, and then the skull is split!
This harness hides, what's more, my notes of
    change,
And in my pockets carry I my gold;
I'll bury that and corse and soul will save
From poverty and death. And if ye mock,
I'll curse you with a patriarchal curse—
With Isaac's curse! O ye, with voices like
The voice of Jacob, but with Esau's hands,
Invert the law of primogeniture!
Myself, my care! What care I more for you!
Hark!

RACHEL.   What noise?

ESTHER.   The drawbridge has been raised—
And now our refuge is a prison too.—

RACHEL. A token that the King has left these walls.
So hastes he forth.—Will he return again?
I fear me no—I fear the very worst!

(Sinking on Esther's breast.)
And yet I loved him truly, loved him well!

ACT IV

A large room with a throne in the foreground to the right. Next to the throne, and running in a straight row to the left, several chairs upon which eight or ten Castilian grandees are sitting. Close to the throne, Manrique de Lara, who has arisen.

MANRIQUE. In sadness we are now assembled here,
But few of us, whom close proximity
Allowed to gather in so short a time.
There will be more to join us presently.
Stern, universal need, delaying not,
Commands us count ourselves as competent.
Before all others, in our earnest group,
Is missing he to whom belongs the right
To call this parliament and here preside;
We then are half illegal at the start.
And so, my noble lords, I took the care
To ask her royal majesty, the Queen,
Although our business much concerns herself,
Here to convene with us and take her place,
That we may know we are not masterless,
Nor feel 'tis usurpation brought us here.
The subject of our council at this time I hope —
I fear — is known to all too well.
The King, our mighty sov'reign — not alone
In rank, estate, and dignity he's high,
But, too, in natural gifts, that when we gaze
Behind us in the past's wide-open book,
We scarce again can find his equal there —

Except that strength, the lever of all good,
When wandered from her wonted path of good,
Wills e'er to do her will with equal strength—
The King, I say, withdraws himself from court,
Lured by a woman's too lascivious charm,
A thing in no wise seeming us to judge—
The Queen!

*The Queen, accompanied by Doña Clara and several
ladies, enters from the right, and seats herself on the
throne, after she has indicated to the grandees who have
arisen that they are to resume their seats.*

MANRIQUE.   Have I permission, Majesty?

QUEEN. Proceed.

MANRIQUE.   What I just said, I shall repeat:
"A thing in no wise seeming us to judge."
But at the bound'ries arms him now the Moor,
And threats with war the hard-oppressed land;
So now the right and duty of the King
Is straight to ward this danger from us all,
With forces he has called and raised himself.
But see, the King is missing! He will come,
I know, if only angry that we called
Of our own power and will this parliament.
But if the cause remains that keeps him hence,
Unto his former bonds he will return,
And, first as last, we be an orphan land.
Your pardon?

[The Queen signs him to continue.]

          First of all, the girl must go.
Full many propositions are at hand.
Some are there here who wish to buy her off,

And others wish to send her from the land,
A prisoner in some far distant clime.
The King has money, too, and though she's far,
You know that power can find whate'er it seeks.
A third proposal—

[The Queen, at these words, has arisen.]

Pardon, noble Queen!
You are too mild for this our business drear!
Your very kindness, lacking vigorous will
From which to draw renewal of its strength,
Has most of all, perhaps, estranged our King.
I blame you not, I say but what is true.
I pray you, then, to waive your own desire,
But if it please you otherwise, then speak!
What flow'ry fate, what flatt'ring punishment,
Is suited to the sin this drab has done?

QUEEN *(softly)*. Death.

MANRIQUE.   In truth?

QUEEN *(more firmly)*.   Yes, death.

MANRIQUE.   Ye hear, my lords!
This was the third proposal, which, although
A man, I did not earlier dare to speak.

QUEEN. Is marriage not the very holiest,
Since it makes right what else forbidden is,
And that, which horrible to all the chaste,
Exalts to duty, pleasing unto God?
Other commandments of our God most high
Give added strength to our regard for right,
But what so strong that it ennobles sin
Must be the strongest of commandments all.
Against that law this woman now has sinned.

But if my husband's wrong continueth,
Then I myself, in all my married years,
A sinner was and not a wife, our son
Is but a misborn bastard-spawn, a shame
Unto himself, and sore disgrace to us.
If ye in me see guilt, then kill me, pray!
I will not live if I be flecked with sin.
Then may he from the princesses about
A spouse him choose, since only his caprice,
And not what is allowed, can govern him.
But if she is the vilest of this earth,
Then purify your King and all his land.
I am ashamed to speak like this to men,
It scarce becomes me, but I needs must speak.

MANRIQUE. But will the King endure this? If so, how?

QUEEN. He will, indeed, because he ought and must.
Then on the murd'rers he can take revenge,
And first of all strike me and this, my breast.

[She sits down.]

MANRIQUE. There is no hope of any other way.
The noblest in the battle meet their doom —
To die a bitter, yea, a cruel death —
Tortured with thirst, and under horses' hoofs,
A doubler, sharper, bitt'rer meed of pain
Than ever sinner on the gallows-tree,
And sickness daily takes our best away;
For God is prodigal with human life;
Should we be timid, then, where his command,
His holy law, which he himself has giv'n,
Demands, as here, that he who sins shall die?
Together then, we will request the King
To move from out his path this stumbling-block

Which keeps him from his own, his own from him.
If he refuse, blood's law be on the land,
Until the law and prince be one again,
And we may serve them both by serving one.

A servant comes.

SERVANT. Don Garceran!

MANRIQUE. And does the traitor dare?

Tell him —

SERVANT. The message is his Majesty's.

MANRIQUE. That's diff'rent. An' he were my deadly
   foe,

He has my ear, when speaks he for the King.

Enter Garceran.

MANRIQUE. At once your message give us; then,
   farewell.

GARCERAN. O Queen, sublime, and thou my father,
   too,

And ye besides, the best of all the land!
I feel today, as ne'er before I felt,
That to be trusted is the highest good,
And that frivolity, though free of guilt,
Destroys and paralyzes more than sin
Itself. *One* error is condoned at last,
Frivolity is ever prone to err.
And so, today, though conscious of no fault,
I stand before you sullied, and atone
For youthful heedlessness that passed for wrong.

MANRIQUE. Of that, another time! Your message
   now!

GARCERAN. The King through me dissolves this
parliament.

MANRIQUE. And since he sent frivolity itself
He surely gave some token from his hand,
Some written word as pledge and surety?

GARCERAN. Hot-foot he followeth.

MANRIQUE.   That is enough!
So in the royal name I now dissolve
This parliament. Ye are dismissed. But list
Ye to my wish and my advice: Return
Ye not at once unto your homes, but wait
Ye rather, round about, till it appears
Whether the King will take the task we leave,
Or we must still perform it in his name.
(To Garceran.)
However, you, in princely service skilled,
If spying be your office 'mongst us here,
I beg you tell your King what I advised,
And that th' estates in truth have been dissolved,
But yet are ready to unite for deeds.

GARCERAN. Then once again, before you all, I say
No tort have I in this mad escapade.
As it was chance that brought me from the camp,
So chanced it that the King selected me
To guard this maiden from the people's rage;
And what with warning, reason, argument,
A man may do to ward off ill, although
'Twas fruitless, I admit,—that have I tried.
I should deserve your scorn were this not so.
And Doña Clara, doubly destined mine,
By parents both and by my wish as well,

You need not hang your noble head, for though
Unworthy of you — never worthy, — I
Not less am worthy now than e'er before.
I stand before you here and swear: 'Tis so.

MANRIQUE. If this is so, and thou art still a man,
Be a Castilian now and join with us
To serve thy country's cause as we it serve.
Thou art acquainted in the castle there;
The captain opes the gates if thou demand.
Perhaps we soon shall need to enter thus,
If deaf the King, our noble lord.

GARCERAN.   No word
Against the King, my master!

MANRIQUE.   Thine the choice!
But follow for the nonce these other lords,
The outcome may be better than we think.

[Servant entering from the left.]

SERVANT. His Majesty, the King!

MANRIQUE *(to the estates, pointing to the middle door).*
                                        This way — withdraw!
(To the servants.)
And ye, arrange these chairs along the wall.
Naught shall remind him that we gathered here.

QUEEN *(who has stepped down from the throne).*
My knees are trembling, yet there's none to aid.

MANRIQUE. Virtue abode with strength in days of
    yore,
But latterly, estranged, they separate.
Strength stayed with youth — where she was wont
    to be —

And virtue fled to gray and ancient heads.
Here, take my arm! Though tottering the step,
And strength be lacking, — virtue still abides.

*[He leads the Queen off at the right. The estates, with
Garceran, have gone out through the centre door. The
King comes from the left, behind him his page.]*

KING. The sorrel, say you, limps? The pace was fast,
But I no further need shall have of him.
So to Toledo, pray you, have him led,
Where rest will soon restore him. I, myself,
Will at my spouse's side, in her own coach
Return from here, in sight of all the folk,
That what they see they may believe, and know
That discord and dissension are removed.

[The page goes.]

I am alone. Does no one come to meet?
Naught but bare walls and silent furniture!
It is but recently that they have met.
And oh, these empty chairs much louder speak
Than those who sat upon them e'er have done!
What use to chew the bitter cud of thought?
I must begin to remedy the ill.
Here goes the way to where my wife doth dwell. —
I'll enter on this most unwelcome path.

[He approaches the side door at the right.]

What, barred the door? Hallo, in there! The King
It is, who's master in this house! For me
There is no lock, no door to shut me out.

[A waiting-woman enters through the door.]

KING. Ye bar yourselves?

WAITING WOMAN.   The Queen, your Majesty —
(As the King is about to enter rapidly.)
The inner door she, too, herself, has locked.

KING. I will not force my way. Announce to her
That I am back, and this my summons is —
Say, rather, my request — as now I say.

[Exit waiting-woman.]

KING *(standing opposite the throne).*
Thou lofty seat, o'ertopping others all,
Grant that we may no lower be than thou,
And even unexalted by these steps
We yet may hold just measure of the good.

Enter the Queen.

KING *(going toward her with outstretched hands).*
I greet thee, Leonore!

QUEEN.   Be welcome, thou!

KING. And not thy hand?

QUEEN.   I'm glad to see thee here.

KING. And not thy hand?

QUEEN *(bursting into tears).* O help me, gracious God!

KING. This hand is not pest-stricken, Leonore,
Go I to battle, as I ought and must,
It will be smeared and drenched with hostile blood;
Pure water will remove the noisome slime,
And for thy "welcome" I shall bring it pure.
Like water for the gross and earthly stain
There is a cleanser for our sullied souls.
Thou art, as Christian, strong enough in faith
To know repentance hath a such-like might.

We others, wont to live a life of deeds,
Are not inclined to modest means like this,
Which takes the guilt away, but not the harm —
Yes, half but is the fear of some new sin.
If wishing better things, if glad resolve
Are any hostage-bond for now and then,
Take it — as I do give it — true and whole!

QUEEN *(holding out both hands).*
O God, how gladly!

KING.   No, not both thy hands!
The right alone, though farther from the heart,
Is giv'n as pledge of contract and of bond,
Perhaps to indicate that not alone
Emotion, which is rooted in our hearts,
But reason, too, the person's whole intent,
Must give endurance to the plighted word.
Emotion's tide is swift of change as time;
That which is pondered, has abiding strength.

QUEEN *(offering him her right hand).*
That too! Myself entire!

KING.   Trembleth thy hand!
(Dropping her hand.)
O noble wife, I would not treat thee ill.
Believe not that, because I speak less mild,
I know less well how great has been my fault,
Nor honor less the kindness of thy heart.

QUEEN. 'Tis easy to forgive; to comprehend
Is much more difficult. How it *could* be,
I understand it not!

KING.   My wife and queen,
We lived as children till but recently.

As such our hands were joined in marriage vows,
And then as guileless children lived we on.
But children grow, with the increase of years,
And ev'ry stage of our development
By some discomfort doth proclaim itself.
Often it is a sickness, warning us
That we are diff'rent — other, though the same,
And other things are fitting in the same.
So is it with our inmost soul as well —
It stretches out, a wider orbit gains,
Described about the selfsame centre still.
Such sickness have we, then, but now passed
      through;
And saying we, I mean that thou as well
Art not a stranger to such inner growth.
Let's not, unheeding, pass the warning by!
In future let us live as kings should live —
For kings we are. Nor let us shut ourselves
From out this world, and all that's good and great;
And like the bees which, at each close of day,
Return unto their hives with lading sweet,
So much the richer by their daily gain,
We'll find within the circle of our home,
Through hours of deprivation, added sweets.

QUEEN. If thou desirest, yes; for me, I miss them not.

KING. But thou wilt miss them then in retrospect,
When thou hast that whereby one judges worth.
But let us now forget what's past and gone!
I like it not, when starting on a course,
By any hindrance thus to bar the way
With rubbish from an earlier estate.

I do absolve myself from all my sins.
Thou hast no need — thou, in thy purity!

QUEEN. Not so! Not so! My husband, if thou
    knew'st
What black and mischief-bringing thoughts have
    found
Their way into my sad and trembling heart!

KING. Perhaps of vengeance? Why, so much the
    better!
Thou feel'st the human duty to forgive,
And know'st that e'en the best of us may err.
We will not punish, nor avenge ourselves;
For *she,* believe me, *she* is guiltless quite,
As common grossness or vain weakness is,
Which merely struggles not, but limply yields.
I only bear the guilt, myself alone.

QUEEN. Let me believe what keeps and comforts me:
The Moorish folk, and all that like them are,
Do practise secret and nefarious arts,
With pictures, signs and sayings, evil draughts,
Which turn a mortal's heart within his breast,
And make his will obedient to their own.

KING. Magic devices round about us are,
But we are the magicians, we ourselves.
That which is far removed, a thought brings near;
What we have scorned, another time seems fair;
And in this world so full of miracles,
We are the greatest miracle ourselves!

QUEEN. She has thy picture!

KING.   And she shall return't,
In full view I shall nail it to the wall,

And for my children's children write beneath:
A King, who, not so evil in himself,
Hath once forgot his office and his duty.
Thank God that he did find himself again.

QUEEN. But thou, thyself, dost wear about thy
  neck —

KING.   Oh yes! Her picture? So you knew that, too?

*[He takes the picture with the chain from his neck, and
lays it on the table in the foreground to the right.]*

So then I lay it down, and may it lie —
A bolt not harmful, now the thunder's past.
The girl herself — let her be ta'en away!
She then may have a man from out her race —

*[Walking fitfully back and forth from the rear to the
front of the stage, and stopping short now and then.]*

But no, not that! — The women of this race
Are passable, good even, but the men
With dirty hands and narrow greed of gain —
This girl shall not be touched by such a one.
Indeed, she has to better ones belonged.
But then, what's that to me! — If thus or thus,
If near or far — they may look after that!

QUEEN. Wilt thou, then, Don Alfonso, stay thus
  strong?

KING *(standing still)*.
Forsooth, thou ne'er hast known or seen this girl!
Take all the faults that on this broad earth dwell,
Folly and vanity, and weakness, too,
Cunning and boldness, coquetry and greed —
Put them together and thou hast this woman;

And if, enigma thou, not magic art,
Shouldst call her power to charm me, I'll agree,
And were ashamed, were't not but natural, too!

QUEEN (walks up and down).
Believe me, husband, 'twas not natural!

KING (standing still).
Magic there is, in truth. Its name is custom,
Which first not potent, later holds us fast;
So that which at the outset shocked, appalled,
Sloughs off the first impression of disgust,
And grows, a thing continued, to a need —
Is this not of our very bodies true!
This chain I wore — which now here idly lies,
Ta'en off forever — breast and neck alike,
To this impression have become so used —
(Shaking himself.)
The empty spaces make me shake with cold.
I'll choose myself another chain forthwith;
The body jests not when it warning sends.
And now enough of this! But that you could
Avenge yourselves in blood on this poor fool —
That was not well!
(Stepping to the table.)
                    For do but see these eyes —
Yes, see the eyes, the body, neck, and form!
God made them verily with master hand;
'Twas she *herself* the image did distort.
Let us revere in her, then, God's own work,
And not destroy what he so wisely built.

QUEEN. Oh, touch it not!

KING.   This nonsense now again!
And if I really take it in my hand,

(He has taken the picture in his hand)
Am I another, then? I wind the chain
In jest, to mock you, thus about my neck.
(Doing it.)
The face that 'frights you in my bosom hide —
Am I the less Alfonso, who doth see
That he has err'd, and who the fault condemns?
Then of your nonsense let this be enough!

[He draws away from the table.]

QUEEN. Only —

KING *(wildly looking at her).*
　　　　　　　　What is't?

QUEEN. 　　　　　　　　O God in heav'n!

KING. Be frighted not, good wife! Be sensible!
Repeat not evermore the selfsame thing!
It doth remind me of the difference.
(Pointing to the table, then to his breast.)
This girl there — no, of course now she is here —
If she was foolish, foolish she would be,
Nor claimed that she was pious, chaste, and wise.
And this is ever virtuous women's way —
They reckon always with their virtue thus;
If you are sad, with virtue comfort they,
If joyous is your mood, virtue again,
To take your cheerfulness at last away,
And show you as your sole salvation, sin.
Virtue's a name for virtues manifold,
And diff'rent, as occasion doth demand —
It is no empty image without fault,
And therefore, too, without all excellence.
I will just doff the chain now from my neck,

For it reminds me — And, then, Leonore,
That with the vassals thou didst join thyself —
That was not well, was neither wise nor just.
If thou art angry with me, thou art right;
But these men, my dependents, subjects all —
What want they, then? Am I a child, a boy,
Who not yet knows the compass of his place?
They share with me the kingdom's care and toil,
And equal care is duty, too, for me.
But I the *man* Alfonso, not the King,
Within my house, my person, and my life —
Must I accounting render to these men?
Not so! And gave I ear but to my wrath,
I quickly would return from whence I came,
To show that they with neither blame nor praise
Shall dare to sit in judgment over me.

[Stepping forward and stamping on the floor.]

And finally this dotard, Don Manrique,
If he was once my guardian, is he still?

*[Don Manrique appears at the centre door. The Queen
points to the King, and wrings her hand. Manrique
withdraws with a reassuring gesture.]*

KING. Presumes he to his sov'reign to prescribe
The rustic precepts of senility?
Would he with secret, rash, and desp'rate deed —
(Walking back and forth diagonally across the stage)
I will investigate this case as judge;
And if there be a trace here of offense,
Of insolent intent or wrongful act,
The nearer that the guilty stand to me,
The more shall boldness pay the penalty.
Not thou, Leonore, no, thou art excused!

*[During the last speech, the Queen has quietly
withdrawn through the door at the right.]*

Whither, then, went she? Leave they me alone?
Am I a fool within mine own abode?

[He approaches the door at the right.]

I'll go to her — What, is it bolted, barred?

[Bursting open the door with a kick.]

I'll take by storm, then, my domestic bliss.

[He goes in.]

*[Don Manrique and Garceran appear at the centre door.
The latter takes a step across the threshold.]*

MANRIQUE. Wilt thou with, us?

GARCERAN.   My father!

MANRIQUE.   Wilt thou not?
The rest are gone — wilt follow them?

GARCERAN.   I will.

*[They withdraw, the door closes. Pause. The King
returns. In the attitude of one listening intently.]*

KING. Listen again! — 'Tis nothing, quiet all! —
Empty, forlorn, the chambers of the Queen.
But, on returning, in the turret room,
I heard the noise of carriages and steeds,
In rushing gallop, hurrying away.
Am I alone? Ramiro! Garceran!

[The page comes from the door at the right.]

KING. Report! What goes on here?

PAGE.   Illustrious Sire,
The castle is deserted; you and I
Are at this hour its sole inhabitants.

KING. The Queen?

PAGE.   The castle in her carriage left.

KING. Back to Toledo then?

PAGE.   I know not, Sire.
The lords, howe'er —

KING.   What lords?

PAGE.   Sire, the estates,
Who all upon their horses swung themselves;
They did not to Toledo take their way —
Rather the way which you yourself did come.

KING. What! To Retiro? Ah, now fall the scales
From these my seeing and yet blinded eyes!
Murder this is. They go to slay her there!
My horse! My horse!

PAGE.   Your horse, illustrious Sire,
Was lame, and, as you know, at your command —

KING. Well, then, another — Garceran's, or yours!
PAGE. They've taken every horse from here away,
Perhaps with them, perhaps but driv'n afar;
As empty as the castle are the stalls.

KING. They think they will outstrip me. But away!
Get me a horse, were't only some old nag;
Revenge shall lend him wings, that he may fly.
And if 'tis done? Then, God above, then grant
That as a man, not as a tyrant, I
May punish both the guilty and the guilt.

71

Get me a horse! Else art thou in their league,
And payest with thy head, as all shall—
(Standing at the door, with a gesture of violence.)
                                                All!

[He hastens away.]

ACT V

A large room in the castle at Retiro, with one door in
the centre and one at each side. Everywhere signs of
destruction. In the foreground, at the left, an overturned
toilet table with scattered utensils. In the background, at
the left, another overturned table; above it a picture half
torn from its frame. In the centre of the room, a chair.
It is dark. From without, behind the middle wall, the
sound of voices, footsteps, and the clatter of weapons,
finally, from without – "It is enough! The signal
sounds! To horse!" Sounds of voices and footsteps die
out. Pause. Then Isaac comes from the door at the right,
dragging along a carpet, which is pulled over his head,
and which he later drops.

ISAAC.   Are they then gone? – I hear no sound.
(Stepping back.)

But yes –

No, no, 'tis naught! When they, a robber band,
Searched all the castle through, I hid myself,
And on the ground all doubled up I lay.
This cover here was roof and shield alike.
But whither now? Long since I hid full well
Here in the garden what I saved and gained;
I'll fetch it later when this noise is past. –
Where is the door? How shall I save my soul?

ESTHER *enters from the door at the left.*

ISAAC.   Who's there? Woe's me!

ESTHER.   Is't thou?

Isaac.   Is't thou, then, Rachel?

Esther. What mean'st thou? Rachel? Only Esther, I!

Isaac. Only, thou say'st? Thou art my only child —
Only, because the best.

Esther.   Nay, rather say,
The best because the only. Aged man,
Dost thou, then, nothing know of this attack,
Nor upon whom they meant to vent their wrath?

Isaac. I do not know, nor do I wish to know,
For has not Rachel flown, to safety gone?
Oh, she is clever, she! — God of my fathers!
Why dost thou try me — me, a poor old man,
And speak to me from out my children's mouths?
But I believe it not! 'Tis false! No, no!

*[He sinks down beside the chair in the centre, leaning
his head against it.]*

Esther. So then be strong through coward
    fearsomeness.
Yet call I others what I was myself.
For when their coming roused me from my sleep,
And I went hurrying to my sister's aid,
Into the last, remote, and inmost room,
One of them seizes me with powerful hand,
And hurls me to the ground. And coward, I,
I fall a-swooning, when I should have stood
And offered up my life to save my sister,
Or, at the very least, have died with her!
When I awoke, the deed was done, and vain
My wild attempt to bring her back to life.
Then could I weep, then could I tear my hair;
That is, indeed, true cowardice, a woman's.

ISAAC. They tell me this and that. But 'tis not true!

ESTHER. Lend me thy chair to sit upon, old man!

[She pulls the chair forward.]

My limbs grow weak and tremble under me.
Here will I sit and here will I keep watch.

[She sits down.]

Mayhap that one will think it worth his while
To burn the stubble, now the harvest's o'er,
And will return and kill what still is left.

ISAAC *(from the floor).* Not me! Not me! — Some one
    is coming. Hark!
No, many come! — Save me — I flee to thee!

[He runs to her chair, and cowers on the floor.]

ESTHER. I like a mother will protect thee now,
The second childhood of the gray old man.
And, if death comes, then childless shalt thou die —
I following Rachel in advance of thee!

*The King appears at the centre door, with his page, who
carries a torch.*

KING. Shall I go farther, or content myself
With what I know, though still it is unseen?
This castle all a-wreck, laid bare and waste,
Shrieking from ev'ry corner cries to me
It is too late, the horror has been done!
And thou the blame must bear, cursed dallier,
If not, forsooth, a party to the deed!
But no, thou weepst, and tears no lies can tell.
Behold, I also weep, I weep for rage,
From hot and unslaked passion for revenge!
Come, here's a ring to set your torch within.

Go to the town, assemble all the folk,
And bid them straight unto this castle come
With arms, as chance may put within their reach;
And I, when morning comes, with written word,
Will bring the people here, at my command —
Children of toil and hard endeavor, they,
As an avenger at their head I'll go,
And break down all the strongholds of the great,
Who, half as servants, half again as lords,
Serve but themselves and overrule their master.
Ruler and ruled, thus shall it be, and I,
Avenging, will wipe out that hybrid throng,
So proud of blood, or flowing in their veins,
Or dripping on their swords from others' wounds.
Thy light here leave and go! I'll stay alone
And hatch the progeny of my revenge.

*[The servant puts his torch into the ring beside the
door and withdraws.]*

KING *(taking a step forward)*. What moves there!
   Can it be there still is life?
Give answer!

ISAAC.   Gracious Lord ill-doer, O,
O, spare us, good assassin!

KING.   You, old man?
Remind me not that Rachel was your child;
It would deface her image in my soul.
And thou — art thou not Esther?

ESTHER.   Sire, I am.

KING. And is it done?

ESTHER.   It is.

KING.   I knew it well,
Since I the castle entered. So, no plaints!
For know, the cup is full; an added drop
Would overflow, make weak the poisonous
    draught.
While she still lived I was resolved to leave her,
Now dead, she ne'er shall leave my side again;
And this her picture, here upon my breast,
Will 'grave its image there, strike root within—
For was not mine the hand that murdered her?
Had she not come to me, she still would play,
A happy child, a joy to look upon.
Perhaps—but no, not that! No, no, I say!
No other man should ever touch her hand,
No other lips approach her rosy mouth,
No shameless arm—she to the King belonged,
Though now unseen, she still would be my own.
To royal might belongs such might of charms!

ISAAC. Speaks he of Rachel?

ESTHER.   Of thy daughter, yes
Though grief increase the value of the loss,
Yet must I say: Too high you rate her worth.

KING. Think'st thou? I tell thee, naught but
    shadows we—
I, thou, and others of the common crowd;
For if thou'rt good, why then, thou'st learned it so;
If I am honest, I but saw naught else;
Those others, if they murder,—as they do—
Well, so their fathers did, came time and need!
The world is but one great reechoing,
And all its harvest is but seed from seed.
But she was truth itself, ev'n though deformed,

And all she did proceeded from herself,
A-sudden, unexpected, and unlearned.
Since her I saw I felt myself alive,
And to the dreary sameness of my life
'T was only she gave character and form.
They tell that in Arab desert wastes
The wand'rer, long tormented in the sands,
Long tortured with the sun's relentless glare,
Some time may find a blooming island's green,
Surrounded by the surge of arid waves;
There flowers bloom, there trees bestow their shade,
The breath of herbs mounts soothing in the breeze
And forms a second heav'n, arched 'neath the first.
Forsooth the serpent coils among the brush;
A famished beast, tormented by like thirst,
Perchance comes, too, to slake it at this spring;
Yet, tired and worn, the wand'rer doth rejoice,
Sucks in with greedy lips the cooling draught,
And sinks down in the rank luxuriant growth.
Luxuriant growth! In faith! I'll see her now —
See once again that proud and beauteous form,
That mouth which drew in breath and breathed
    out life,
And which, now silenced ever, evermore,
Accuses me of guarding her so ill.

ESTHER. Go not, O Sire! Now that the deed is done,
Let it be done. The mourning be for us!
Estrange thyself not from thy people, Sire.

KING. Think'st thou? The King I am — thou know'st
full well.
She suffered outrage, but myself no less.
Justice, and punishment of ev'ry wrong

I swore upon my coronation day,
And I will keep my oath until the death.
To do this, I must make me strong and hard,
For to my anger they will sure oppose
All that the human breast holds high and dear—
Mem'ries from out my boyhood's early days,
My manhood's first sweet taste of woman's love,
Friendship and gratitude and mercy, too;
My whole life, roughly bundled into one,
Will stand, as 't were against me, fully armed,
And challenge me to combat with myself.
I, therefore, from myself must first take leave.
Her image, as I see it here and there,
On every wall, in this and every corner
Shows her to me but in her early bloom,
With all her weaknesses, with all her charm.
I'll see her now, mistreated, wounded, torn;
Will lose myself in horror at the sight,
Compare each bloody mark upon her form
With this, her image, here upon my breast.
And learn to deal with monsters, like to like.
(As Esther has risen.)
Speak not a word to me! I will! This torch
Shall, like myself, inflamed, illume the way;
Gleaming, because destructive and destroyed.
She is in yonder last and inmost room,
Where I so oft—

ESTHER.   She was, and there remains.

KING *(has seized the torch)*. Methinks 'tis blood I see
      upon my way.
It is the way to blood. O fearful night!

[He goes out at the side door to the left.]

ISAAC. We're in the dark.

ESTHER.   Yes, dark is round about,
And round about the horror's horrid night.
But daylight comes apace. So let me try
If I can thither bear my weary limbs.

[She goes to the window, and draws the curtain.]

The day already dawns, its pallid gleam
Shudders to see the terrors wrought this night—
The difference 'twixt yesterday and now.
(Pointing to the scattered jewels on the floor.)
There, there it lies, our fortune's scattered ruin—
The tawdry baubles, for the sake of which
We, we—not he who takes the blame—but we
A sister sacrificed, thy foolish child!
Yea, all that comes is right. Whoe'er complains,
Accuses his own folly and himself.

ISAAC *(who has seated himself on the chair).*
Here will I sit. Now that the King is here
I fear them not, nor all that yet may come.

*The centre door opens. Enter Manrique and Garceran,
behind them the Queen, leading her child by the hand,
and other nobles.*

MANRIQUE. Come, enter here, arrange yourselves
    the while.
We have offended 'gainst his Majesty,
Seeking the good, but not within the law.
We will not try now to evade the law.

ESTHER *(on the other side, raising the overturned table
with a quick movement).* Order thyself, disorder!
    Lest they think
That we are terrified, or cowards prove.

QUEEN. Here are those others, here.

MANRIQUE.   Nay, let them be!
What mayhap threatens us, struck them ere now.
I beg you, stand you here, in rank and file.

QUEEN. Let me come first, I am the guiltiest!

MANRIQUE. Not so. O Queen. Thou spak'st the
      word, 'tis true,
But when it came to action thou didst quake,
Oppose the deed, and mercy urge instead,
Although in vain; for need became our law.
Nor would I wish the King's first burst of rage
To strike the mighty heads we most revere
As being next to him, the Kingdom's hope.
I did the deed, not with this hand, forsooth—
With counsel, and with pity, deep and dread!
The first place, then, is mine. And thou, my son—
Hast thou the heart to answer like a man
For that which at the least thou hinder'dst not,
So that thy earnest wish to make amends
And thy return have tangled thee in guilt!

GARCERAN. Behold me ready! To your side I come!
And may the King's first fury fall on me!

ESTHER *(calling across)*. You there, although all
      murderers alike,
Deserving every punishment and death—
Enough of mischief is already done,
Nor would I wish the horrors yet increased!
Within, beside my sister, is the King;
Enraged before he went, the sight of her
Will but inflame his passionate ire anew.
I pity, too, that woman and her child,

Half innocent, half guilty — only half.
So go while yet there's time, and do not meet
Th' avenger still too hot to act as judge.

MANRIQUE. Woman, we're Christians!

ESTHER.   You have shown you are.
Commend me to the Jewess, O my God!

MANRIQUE. Prepared as Christians, too, to expiate
In meek submission all of our misdeeds.
Lay off your swords. Here now is first my own!
To be in armor augurs of defense.
Our very number makes submission less.
Divide we up the guilt each bears entire.

[All have laid their swords on the floor before Manrique.]

So let us wait. Or rather, let one go
To urge upon the King most speedily,
The country's need demands, this way or that,
That he compose himself; and though it were
Repenting a rash deed against ourselves!
Go thou, my son!

GARCERAN *(turning around after having taken several steps).* Behold, the King himself!

[The King rushes out of the apartment at the side. After taking a few steps, he turns about and stares fixedly at the door.]

QUEEN. O God in Heaven!

MANRIQUE.   Queen, I pray be calm!

[The King goes toward the front. He stops, with arms folded, before old Isaac, who lies back as if asleep, in the armchair. Then he goes forward.]

ESTHER *(to her father)*. Behold thy foes are trembling!
   Art thou glad?
Not I. For Rachel wakes not from the dead.

*[The King, in the front, gazes at his hands, and rubs
them, as though washing them, one over the other.
Then the same motion over his body. At last he feels his
throat, moving his hands around it. In this last position,
with his hands at his throat, he remains motionless,
staring fixedly before him.]*

MANRIQUE. Most noble Prince and King. Most
   gracious Sire!

KING *(starting violently)*. Ye here? 'Tis good ye
come! I sought for you —
And all of you. Ye spare me further search.

*[He steps before them, measuring them with angry
glances.]*

MANRIQUE *(pointing to the weapons lying on the floor)*.
We have disarmed ourselves, laid down our swords.

KING. I see the swords. Come ye to slay me, then!
I pray, complete your work. Here is my breast!

[He opens his robe.]

QUEEN. He has't no more!

KING.   How mean you, lady fair?

QUEEN. Gone is the evil picture from his neck

KING. I'll fetch it, then.

*[He takes a few steps toward the door at the side, and
then stands still.]*

QUEEN.   O God, this madness still!

MANRIQUE. We know full well, how much we, Sire,
    have erred —
Most greatly, that we did not leave to thee
And thine own honor thy return to self!
But, Sire, the time more pressing was than we.
The country trembled, and at all frontiers
The foemen challenged us to ward our land.

KING. And foemen must be punished — is't not so?
Ye warn me rightly; I am in their midst.
Ho, Garceran!

GARCERAN.   Thou meanest me, O Sire?

KING. Yea, I mean, thee! Though me thou hast
    betrayed,
Thou wert my friend. Come to me then, I say,
And tell me what thou think'st of her within!
Her — whom thou help'dst to slay — of that anon.
What thoughtst thou of her while she still did live?

GARCERAN. O Sire, I thought her fair.

KING.   What more was she?

GARCERAN. But wanton, too, and light, with evil
    wiles.

KING. And that thou hidst from me while still was
    time?

GARCERAN. I said it, Sire!

KING.   And I believed it not?
How came that? Pray, say on!

GARCERAN.   My Sire — the Queen,
She thinks't was magic.

KING.   Superstition, bah!
Which fools itself with idle make-believe.

GARCERAN. In part, again, it was but natural.

KING. That only which is right is natural.
And was I not a king, both just and mild —
The people's idol and the nobles', too?
Not empty-minded, no, and, sure, not blind!
I say, she was not fair!

GARCERAN.   How meanest, Sire ?

KING. An evil line on cheek and chin and mouth.
A lurking something in that fiery glance
Envenom'd and disfigured all her charm.
But erst I've gazed upon it and compared.
When there I entered in to fire my rage,
Half fearsome of the mounting of my ire,
It happened otherwise than I had thought.
Instead of wanton pictures from the past,
Before my eyes came people, wife, and child.
With that her face seemed to distort itself,
The arms to rise, to grasp me, and to hold.
I cast her likeness from me in the tomb
And now am here, and shudder, as thou seest.
But go thou now! For, hast thou not betrayed me?
Almost I rue that I must punish you.
Go thither to thy father and those others —
Make no distinction, ye are guilty, all.

MANRIQUE *(with a strong voice)*. And thou?

KING *(after a pause)*. The man is right; I'm guilty, too.
But what is my poor land, and what the world,
If none are pure, if malefactors all!
Nay, here's my son. Step thou within our midst!

Thou shalt be guardian spirit of this land;
Perhaps a higher judge may then forgive.
Come, Doña Clara, lead him by the hand!
Benignant fortune hath vouchsafed to thee
In native freedom to pursue thy course
Until this hour; thou, then, dost well deserve
To guide the steps of innocence to us.
But hold! Here is the mother. What she did,
She did it for her child. She is forgiv'n!

[As the Queen steps forward and bends her knee.]

Madonna, wouldst thou punish me? Wouldst show
The attitude most seeming me toward thee?
Castilians all, behold! Here is your King,
And here is she, the regent in his stead!
I am a mere lieutenant for my son.
For as the pilgrims, wearing, all, the cross
For penance journey to Jerusalem,
So will I, conscious of my grievous stain,
Lead you against these foes of other faith
Who at the bound'ry line, from Africa,
My people threaten and my peaceful land.
If I return, and victor, with God's grace,
Then shall ye say if I am worthy still
To guard the law offended by myself.
This punishment be *yours* as well as mine,
For all of you shall follow me, and first,
Into the thickest squadrons of the foe.
And he who falls does penance for us all.
Thus do I punish you and me! My son
Here place upon a shield, like to a throne,
For he today is King of this our land.
So banded, then, let's go before the folk.

[A shield has been brought.]

You women, each do give the child a hand.
Slipp'ry his first throne, and the second too!
Thou, Garceran, do thou stay at my side,
For equal wantonness we must atone —
So let us fight as though our strength were one.
And hast thou purged thyself of guilt, as I,
Perhaps that quiet, chaste, and modest maid
Will hold thee not unworthy of her hand!
Thou shalt improve him, Doña Clara, but
Let not thy virtue win his mere respect,
But lend it charm, as well. That shields from much.

[Trumpets in the distance.]

Hear ye? They call us. Those whom I did bid
To help against you, they are ready all
To help against the common enemy,
The dreaded Moor who threats our boundaries,
And whom I will send back with shame and wounds
Into the arid desert he calls home,
So that our native land be free from ill,
Well-guarded from within and from without.
On, on! Away! God grant, to victory!

*[The procession has already formed. First, some vassals,
then the shield with the child, whom the women hold by
both hands, then the rest of the men Lastly, the King,
leaning in a trustful manner on Garceran.]*

ESTHER *(turning to her father).* Seest thou, they are
    already glad and gay;
Already plan for future marriages!
They are the great ones, for th' atonement feast
They've slain as sacrifice a little one,
And give each other now their bloody hands.

[Stepping to the centre.]

But this I say to thee, thou haughty King,
Go, go, in all thy grand forgetfulness!
Thou deem'st thou'rt free now from my sister's
   power,
Because the prick of its impression's dulled,
And thou didst from thee cast what once enticed.
But in the battle, when thy wavering ranks
Are shaken by thy en'mies' greater might,
And but a pure, and strong, and guiltless heart
Is equal to the danger and its threat;
When thou dost gaze upon deaf heav'n above,
Then will the victim, sacrificed to thee,
Appear before thy quailing, trembling soul —
Not in luxuriant fairness that enticed,
But changed, distorted, as she pleased thee not —
Then, pentinent, perchance, thou'lt beat thy breast,
And think upon the Jewess of Toledo!
(Seizing her father by the shoulder.)
Come, father, come! A task awaits us there.

[Pointing to the side door.]

ISAAC *(as though waking from sleep).*
But first I'll seek my gold!

ESTHER.   Think'st still of that
In sight of all this misery and woe?
Then I unsay the curse which I have spoke,
Then thou art guilty, too, and I — and she!
We stand like them within the sinners' row;
Pardon we, then, that God may pardon us!

[With arms outstretched toward the side door.]

CURTAINS

Books published by Mondial

French Classics:

1. Rougon-Macquart Series:

Emile Zola: The Fortune of the Rougons
ISBN 1595690107 / 9781595690104

Emile Zola: The Fat and the Thin (The Belly of Paris)
ISBN 1595690522 / 9781595690524

Emile Zola: Abbe Mouret's Transgression
(The Sin of the Abbé Mouret) ISBN 1595690506 / 9781595690500

Emile Zola: The Dream. ISBN 1595690492 / 9781595690494

Emile Zola: A Love Episode (A Page of Love)
ISBN 1595690271 / 9781595690272

Emile Zola: The Conquest of Plassans
ISBN 1595690484 / 9781595690487

Emile Zola: The Joy of Life (Zest for Life)
ISBN 1595690476 / ISBN 9781595690470

Emile Zola: Doctor Pascal. ISBN 1595690514 / 9781595690517

Emile Zola: His Excellency (His Excellency, Eugène Rougon)
ISBN 1595690557 / 9781595690555

Emile Zola: Money. ISBN 9781595690630

Emile Zola: Piping Hot! (Pot Bouille). *Illustrated Edition.*
ISBN 9781595691231

Emile Zola: The Soil (The Earth). ISBN 9781595690883

Emile Zola: The Downfall (La Debacle). ISBN 9781595691118

2. Other French Literature:

Emile Zola: The Mysteries of Marseille. ISBN 9781595690913

Emile Zola: The Flood. ISBN 9781595690944

Emile Zola: Death. ISBN 9781595690937

Emile Zola: Fruitfulness ISBN 1595690182 / 9781595690180

Emile Zola: For a Night of Love. ISBN 9781595691217

Emile Zola: The Fête in Coqueville
(The Coqueville Spree) ISBN 9781595690869

Emile Zola: Jean Gourdon's Four Days. ISBN 9781595691224

Victor Hugo: Ninety-Three. ISBN 9781595690920

Victor Hugo: Bug-Jargal. ISBN 9781595690951

Victor Hugo: The Man Who Laughs (By Order of the King)
ISBN 1595690131 / 9781595690135

Victor Hugo: History of a Crime.
ISBN 1595690204 / 9781595690203

Voltaire: The Princess of Babylon. ISBN 9781595690999

Honoré de Balzac: Ursula (Ursule Mirouet). ISBN 9781595690531

Honoré de Balzac: Maitre Cornelius. ISBN 9781595690173

Anatole France: Penguin Island.
ISBN 1595690298 / 9781595690296

Anatole France: The Crime of Sylvestre Bonnard
ISBN 9781595690593

Anatole France: The Gods are Athirst (Les Dieux ont soif)
ISBN 9781595690128

Gustave Flaubert: Salammbo (Salambo)
ISBN 1595690352 / 9781595690357

Romain Rolland: Pierre and Luce. ISBN 9781595690609

Romain Rolland: Colas Breugnon. A Burgundian Story.
ISBN 9781595691330

Jules Verne: An Antarctic Mystery (The Sphinx of the Ice Fields)
ISBN 1595690549 / 9781595690548

André Gide: Strait is the Gate (La Porte étroite)
ISBN 9781595690623

André Gide: Prometheus Illbound. ISBN 9781595690807

André Gide: Recollections of Oscar Wilde. ISBN 9781595690814

Alphonse Daudet:
Little What's-His-Name (aka Little Good-for-Nothing)
(Le Petit Chose. French Classics). ISBN 9781595691057

German Classics:

Conrad Ferdinand Meyer: The Monk's Marriage. 9781595691385

Franz Grillparzer: The Jewess of Toledo. ISBN 9781595691392

Franz Grillparzer: The Poor Musician. (Austrian Classics).
ISBN 9781595691095

Heinrich Heine: Germany. A Winter Tale (Deutschland.
Ein Wintermärchen.) Bilingual Edition. ISBN 9781595690715

Heinrich Heine: The Rabbi of Bacharach
(German Classics) ISBN 9781595691002

Heinrich Heine: Florentine Nights.
(German Classics) ISBN 9781595691019

Heinrich Heine: From the Memoirs of Herr von Schnabelewopski
(German Classics) ISBN 9781595691026

Theodor Fontane: Trials and Tribulations. A Berlin Novel
(German Classics) ISBN 9781595691255

Bernhard Kellermann: God's Beloved (Illustrated)
(German Classics) ISBN 9781595691262

Gotthold Ephraim Lessing: Minna von Barnhelm or The Soldier's
Fortune (German Classics). ISBN: 9781595691248

Johann Wolfgang von Goethe: The Sorrows of Young Werther
ISBN 159569045X / 9781595690456
Theodor Storm: The Rider of the White Horse
(The Dikegrave; aka The Dykemaster). ISBN 9781595690746

Heinrich von Kleist: Michael Kohlhaas
(A Tale from an Old Chronicle). ISBN 9781595690760

Gottfried Keller: A Village Romeo and Juliet
(Swiss-German Classics). ISBN 9781595690791

Gottfried Keller: Ursula (Swiss-German Classics).
ISBN 9781595690838

Gottfried Keller: The Governor of Greifensee
(Swiss-German Classics). ISBN 9781595690845

Wilhelm Raabe: The Hunger Pastor
(German Classics). ISBN 9781595690753

Theodor Storm, Adelbert von Chamisso, Adalbert Stifter:
Famous German Novellas of the 19th Century (Immensee. Peter
Schlemihl. Brigitta.) ISBN 159569014X / 9781595690142

Marie von Ebner-Eschenbach: Krambambuli. The District Doctor
(Two Novellas. Austrian Classics). ISBN 9781595691040

E. T. A. Hoffmann: The Sandman. The Elementary Spirit
(Two Tales. German Classics). ISBN 9781595691170

Wilhelm Hauff: The Cold Heart. Nose, the Dwarf
(Two Tales. German Classics). ISBN 9781595691187

Danish Classics:

Martin Andersen Nexo: Pelle the Conqueror (Complete Edition:
Boyhood. Apprenticeship. The Great Struggle. Daybreak.)
ISBN 159569028X / 9781595690289

Martin Andersen Nexo: Ditte Everywoman (Complete Edition:
Girl Alive. Daughter of Man. Towards the Stars.)
ISBN 9781595690333

Italian Classics:

Gabriele D'Annunzio:
The Child of Pleasure. ISBN 9781595690581

Luigi Pirandello: Signora Speranza. ISBN 9781595691088:

African Literature:

Malama Katulwende: Bitterness (An African Novel from Zambia)
ISBN 159569031X / 9781595690319

British Classics:

Oscar Wilde: The Critic as Artist. Upon the Importance of Doing
Nothing and Discussing Everything. ISBN 9781595690821

Oscar Wilde, Anonymous: Teleny or The Reverse of the Medal
(Gay erotic classic) ISBN 1595690360 / 9781595690364

H. G. Wells: Tales of Space and Time. ISBN 9781595691220

Rudyard Kipling: Ghost Stories. ISBN 9781595691323

Agatha Christie: Two Novels (The Mysterious Affair at Styles.
The Secret Adversary.) ISBN 1595690417 / 9781595690418

Jerome K. Jerome: Idle Thoughts of an Idle Fellow
ISBN 1595690247 / 9781595690241

Virgina Woolf: Jacob's Room. ISBN 9781595691149

Jane Austen: Persuasion. Northanger Abbey (Two Novels)
ISBN: 9781595691156

William Somerset Maugham: The Trembling of a Leaf.
ISBN 9781595691194

Howard Overing Sturgis: Belchamber. ISBN 9781595691316

Howard Overing Sturgis: All That Was possible.
ISBN 9781595691293

Howard Overing Sturgis: Tim (Gay Classics).
ISBN 9781595691309

US-American Literature:

Jack London: War of the Classes. Revolution. The Shrinkage of the Planet. ISBN 1595690409 / 9781595690401

Jack London: Before Adam. Children of the Frost. ISBN 1595690395 / 9781595690395

Jack London: The Iron Heel. ISBN 1595690379 / 9781595690371

Jack London: Burning Daylight. ISBN 9781595691064

Donald Windham: Two People (Gay Classics). ISBN 9781595691033

Susan Coolidge: Clover. ISBN 1595690263 / 9781595690265

Gertrude Stein: Three Lives (With an Introduction by Carl Van Vechten). ISBN 1595690425 / 9781595690425

Sinclair Lewis: The Trail of the Hawk. ISBN 9781595691132

Carl Van Vechten: Firecrackers. A Realistic Novel. ISBN 9781595690635

Bruce Kellner: Winter Ridge (A Love Story) ISBN 9781595690692

Polish Classics:

Adam Mickiewicz: Pan Tadeusz or The Last Foray in Lithuania (aka Pan Thaddeus / Mister Thaddeus). ISBN 9781595691347

Russian Classics:

Anton Chekhov (Tchekoff): The Lady with the Toy Dog. And Other Famous Short Stories. ISBN 9781595691354

Gay Classics:

Oscar Wilde, Anonymous: Teleny or The Reverse of the Medal (Gay erotic classic) ISBN 1595690360 / 9781595690364

Donald Windham: Two People (Gay Classics). ISBN 9781595691033

Howard Overing Sturgis: Tim (Gay Classics) ISBN 9781595691309

Contemporary Literature:

Bruce Kellner: Winter Ridge. A Love Story. ISBN 9781595690692

Malama Katulwende: Bitterness (An African Novel from Zambia) ISBN 159569031X / 9781595690319

Other Books (Non-Fiction):

Frederick (Friedrich) Engels: Socialism: Utopian and Scientific (Appendix: The Mark; Preface by Karl Marx) ISBN 1595690468 / 9781595690463

Karl Marx: The Eighteenth Brumaire of Louis Bonaparte. ISBN 1595690239 / 9781595690234

Frederick (Friedrich) Engels: Feuerbach — The Roots of the Socialist Philosophy. **Karl Marx:** Theses on Feuerbach ISBN 9781595691286

Sigmund Freud: Dream Psychology (Psychoanalysis for Beginners). ISBN 9781595690166

Carl Van Vechten: Caruso's Moustache Off and Other Writings About Music (Musical Essays). ISBN 9781595690708